HOU MIE

ED OL

ECIAL

S

Check out these other books in the
How I Survived Middle School series by Nancy Krulik:

Krulik

HOW I SURVIVED MIDDLE SCHOOL

SUPER SPECIAL

How the Pops Stole Christmas

By Nancy Krulik

SCHOLASTIC INC.

New York Toronto London Auckland
Sydney Mexico City New Delhi Hong Kong

For Wendy, David, and Alison

No part of this publication may be reproduced, stored in a retrieval system, or transmitted in any form or by any means, electronic, mechanical, photocopying, recording, or otherwise, without written permission of the publisher. For information regarding permission, write to Scholastic Inc., Attention: Permissions Department, 557 Broadway, New York, NY 10012.

ISBN-13: 978-0-545-19760-1
ISBN-10: 0-545-19760-0

12 11 10 9 8 7 6 5 4 3 2 1   9 10 11 12 13 14/0

Printed in the U.S.A.
First printing, October 2009

Are You Santa or Scrooge?

WHEN IT COMES to the holidays, are you better known for your hearty "Ho, ho, ho," or your bummed-out "Bah, humbug"? Are you a brave red-nosed reindeer, or a jolly snowman? To find out which Christmas character you're most like, give this Christmassy quiz a try.

1. What nonmaterial gift do you most want for Christmas?

A. To find the perfect gift for my BFF.
B. To gather everyone I love in one place.
C. Snow.
D. December 26th.

2. How do you like to spread Christmas cheer?

A. By handing out beautifully wrapped gifts.
B. By getting a group of friends together to go caroling.
C. By decorating my house and tree.
D. I'll cheer up the minute Christmas is over.

3. Do you believe in Santa Claus?

A. I believe in the spirit of Santa.
B. Sometimes I find myself believing when I'm around little kids who still believe.
C. No, but it's still fun to tell the mall Santa what I want for Christmas.
D. No way. I'm not five anymore.

4. Which Christmas treat do you think is most like you?

A. Cookies and milk. They're warm and comforting.
B. Chocolates. I like to be surprised when I find out what's inside them.
C. Gingerbread men. They're sweet and spicy at the same time.
D. Carrot sticks. I like to eat healthy.

5. Are you going to any Christmas parties this year?

A. I'm helping out at a party at a homeless shelter.
B. My friends and I are going to lots of parties.
C. I'm throwing the party.
D. No. I'm not the party type.

6. Finish this sentence: To me, it's not Christmas unless:

A. I've found the perfect gift for everyone.
B. The tree is brightly lit.
C. I'm laughing with my BFFs.
D. It's December 25th.

7. On Christmas I like to wear:

A. A red-and-white hat.
B. Anything festive and glittery.
C. A beautiful new scarf.
D. My pajamas.

8. How do you decide what gifts to get your friends?

A. I listen carefully to their hints.
B. I go window shopping until I find something I think they'll like.
C. I get them gift cards so they can pick out something they'll really enjoy.
D. We make a deal not to exchange presents.

Now it's time to add up your answers and figure out which Christmas character you're most like.

Mostly A's: Ho, ho, ho! You're kind, generous, and full of the Christmas spirit. There's no one you could be more like than *Santa Claus*!

Mostly B's: When it comes to shimmery, glimmery, holiday cheer, you're the leader of the pack. You are very much like that shiny star of Santa's sleigh, *Rudolph the Red-Nosed Reindeer*.

Mostly C's: It's clear you are a social person who loves being surrounded by friends during the holiday season. You don't fear a cold winter's night — after all, that's how Christmas is supposed to feel! You're most like *Frosty the Snowman*.

Mostly D's: Bah, humbug! You've got a bad case of the holiday blues, *Mr. Scrooge*. But that can change in an instant. Force yourself to go out and wish everyone you meet a Happy Holiday. You just might discover some Christmas spirit after all.

Chapter ONE

"JINGLE BELLS, *jingle bells, jingle all the way!*"

I think it's impossible not to sing along when I hear Christmas carols playing, which is why I suddenly found myself singing "Jingle Bells" in the middle of our school gym on Monday afternoon. Talk about being totally out of character. I never sing in front of people. At least not usually. But it was Christmastime, and I couldn't help myself.

Of course, I wasn't the only person who was singing along with the holiday CD that was playing. Pretty much everyone in the gym was doing the same thing. That CD was definitely getting everyone in the holiday spirit, which was a good thing. We'd already spent two hours sorting the coat donations we'd received for the annual Joyce Kilmer Middle School charity coat drive, and it was hard work. We needed something to help keep up our energy level.

"*Dashing through the snow, in a one-horse open sleigh*," I sang out joyfully. "*O'er the fields we go, laughing all the way. . . . Ha ha ha . . .*"

"Hey, Jenny, quit howling," Dana Harrison said loudly. She turned to her friend Addie Wilson. "I didn't know they allowed dogs in school," she said.

Addie giggled. "Jenny does sound like a hound dog howling when she sings," she agreed. "She always has."

And that's why I don't sing in front of groups of people. Especially not groups of people that include Addie and Dana. I don't exactly have the world's greatest voice.

"It's better than having a *face* like a hound dog, Addie," my friend Chloe declared, leaping to my defense.

Talk about a major dis! Addie stared at Chloe for a minute. Then she opened her mouth to retaliate. But before she could say a word, Ms. Gold, the school principal, stopped her. Ordinarily Ms. Gold would have been pretty angry with Addie and Chloe for speaking the way they were, but I guess because we were all volunteering our after-school time for the coat drive, she was a little nicer about it. But *just* a little.

"That's enough, ladies," Ms. Gold said firmly. "Joyce Kilmer Middle School students do not *ever* speak to one another that way. Now, let's get back to work. We have a lot of coats to sort, and a lot of cold, homeless families who are waiting for them."

"Yes, ma'am," Chloe murmured quietly.

"Yes, Ms. Gold," Addie said.

As I went back to work, I glanced over in Chloe's direction and mouthed the words, "Thank you."

Chloe shot me a wink and a smile, and then went back to sorting coats. As she separated the girls' coats from the boys', and the grown-ups' coats from the kids' coats, she began to sing along with the Christmas music.

"Rudolph the Red-Nosed Reindeer, had a very shiny nose . . ."

Chloe wasn't afraid of anyone making fun of her as she sang. She happens to have an awesome voice. I shot Chloe another smile. She smiled back, and sang a little louder.

"Please hang any coats that have already been dry-cleaned on the rack," my English teacher, Ms. Jaffe, reminded us. "All other coats have to go into the laundry bags."

Dana held up a blue-and-white ski jacket, and

made a face. "This thing is hideous," she announced. She glanced at the name tag inside. "I should have known. It's Jenny McAfee's old coat."

I could feel a familiar rush of heat heading up into my cheeks, which is what always happens when I start to feel embarrassed. When it comes to blushing, I'm the champion. It doesn't take much to turn me red. For instance, that little obnoxious comment from Dana was about all I needed for my face to turn into one large red tomato with eyes.

"I wonder if I should even bother throwing this thing into the laundry bag," Dana continued, still holding up my old ski jacket. "I mean, it's not like you can dry-clean away geekiness."

Dana's friends, Addie, Claire, Sabrina, and Maya, all began laughing hysterically. Personally, I didn't think it was a particularly funny joke, but then again, I'm not an expert on really mean humor. That's the Pops' territory.

The Pops. That's what my friends and I call the group of kids Dana and Addie hang around with. Pops, as in *pop*ular. Every school has a group just like them. They're the girls who always have the coolest clothes, the newest cell phones, and the best makeup. The Pops are the kids everyone in school would want to be if they could.

But most people *can't* be one of them, because the Pops are a very exclusive group. I should know. I learned that the hard way, during the very first week I was in middle school, when my former friend, Addie Wilson, dumped me to become one of the Pops.

Back in elementary school, Addie and I had been BFFs. Totally. We were never apart. My dad liked to tease us and call us JenAddie McWilson, because we really were like one person. We did everything together. That is, until I spent the summer between elementary school and middle school at sleepaway camp. Addie didn't go to camp with me. Instead, she went to the day camp at the local community center. By the time I got home at the end of the summer, Addie was a Pop and I was . . . well . . . a not. Which explains why right now my former BFF was standing around with the other Pops, laughing at me.

Of course, I have friends, too. Lots of them. And the truth is I'd rather hang around with them than the Pops anytime. My friends aren't back-stabbers. And they don't enjoy being mean to other people. My friends are always there for me when I need them. Which was why at that moment, Chloe, along with our friends Felicia, Rachel, and Sam, were all rushing to my side, making sure my feelings weren't hurt.

"Don't listen to Dana," Felicia told me. "She's just a jerk."

"Exactly," Chloe agreed. "And don't worry. She'll get hers. You know what the song says. 'He knows if you've been bad or good, so be good for goodness' sake.'"

Sam laughed. "Chloe's right. Father Christmas is sure to leave a lump of coal in her stocking this year."

I smiled. I love the way Sam says things. She just moved here from England a few months ago, and she has this great British accent. Sometimes it's almost like we don't speak the same language because she's always using different names for things. Like calling Santa Claus *Father Christmas*, for example.

"Speaking of Santa Claus," Rachel began, a big smile spreading across her face.

"Uh-oh," Felicia said. "I know that smile. There's a joke coming on."

I giggled. I knew exactly what Felicia meant. Rachel always got a goofy smile on her face just before she told us one of her really, really bad jokes.

"Do you guys know where Santa stays when he's on vacation?" Rachel asked us.

"No, where?" Sam asked her.

"At a ho-ho-hotel!" Rachel exclaimed. Then she burst out laughing at her own joke. "Get it?" she asked.

"Oh, I get it, all right," Felicia answered. "And I'm throwing it right back at you."

Rachel knew Felicia was just teasing her. In fact, she laughed even harder at her joke, just to show Felicia how funny it really was.

The rest of us didn't laugh quite as hard. After all, it had been a pretty bad joke. It was a real groaner, actually. Still, Rachel's joke did manage to bring back my good mood. The word *vacation* has that effect on me. Especially *this* vacation. I couldn't wait for my very first middle school winter break to begin. It was going to be so much fun going skating with my friends, shopping at the mall, and seeing every movie at the multiplex. (At least the ones I was allowed to see.) I had a feeling there wasn't going to be one dull or bad moment for the entire break.

Still, before winter break could start, we had to finish sorting the coats in the gym. And we had to get through four more days of school, which is a pretty long time. A lot can happen in four days.

The next morning I arrived bright and early for my English class. I never like being late for class, especially Ms. Jaffe's. If you're late for her class, she embarrasses you in front of everyone. At least that's what she does the first two times. The third time she gives you a silent lunch, which means you have to eat lunch in the front office all by yourself without talking to anyone. And since I only had four days of school left before vacation, I wanted to make sure nothing horrible happened.

But sometimes, there's nothing you can do to stop the horrible stuff from happening. I found that out the minute Ms. Jaffe stepped up in front of the room to start class.

"Good morning," she greeted us. "I have some wonderful news for all of you."

Okay, I admit that didn't sound so horrible. At least not at first. But did you ever notice that when a teacher says something is wonderful, it rarely turns out that way?

"All of the sixth grade English classes will be participating in a Secret Snowflake gift exchange,"

Ms. Jaffe continued. "Each of you will be someone's Secret Snowflake in this class. For the next three days you will give that person a small, handmade gift. However, your identity will be kept secret until the third day. That's when all the Secret Snowflakes will be revealed."

Everyone in the class seemed really excited about the whole Secret Snowflake thing. I could hear them murmuring as Ms. Jaffe explained it. But I was a little worried. I had two good friends in my English class, Sam and Chloe. How was I supposed to choose only one of them to give my gifts to?

A moment later, that problem was solved for me.

"I've placed all of your names in a hat," Ms. Jaffe told us. "I will come by your desks one by one and let you pick out a slip of paper. The person on the paper is the person you will give your Secret Snowflake gifts to. And there will be no trading names. Please don't tell anyone else in the class who you got. Let's keep the *secret* in *Secret Snowflake*."

As Ms. Jaffe walked down the rows with the red hat filled with names, I said a silent little prayer. "Please don't let me get Addie. Please don't let me get Addie." The last thing I wanted was to have to make gifts for my former BFF.

My heart was pounding as Ms. Jaffe approached my desk. "Please don't let me get Addie. Please don't let me get Addie," I continued saying to myself. Slowly I reached my hand into the red hat and pulled out a name.

I didn't open the slip of paper at first. I just sat there for a minute. Then, finally, when I couldn't stand the suspense anymore, I opened the paper.

DANA HARRISON

I stared at the words for a moment. Then I blinked my eyes, hoping they would suddenly, miraculously change. But of course, they didn't. Obviously I'd made a mistake in my silent wish, because the only thing worse than picking Addie's name out of the hat was getting Dana's name instead. How was I supposed to make gifts for someone who thought everything I touched was completely geeky? No matter what I gave her, she was sure to hate it. And she was sure to let everyone in the entire world – or at least the entire sixth grade – know how awful her Secret Snowflake gifts were. Suddenly I wasn't in such a good mood anymore.

But at lunch I was the only one of my friends who wasn't happy. When I got to my regular cafeteria table during fifth period lunch, my friends seemed positively jolly. They were laughing and smiling. They were clearly looking forward to the break. I wanted to go back to feeling that way, too. So I took my seat at the table and tried to push all thoughts of Dana Harrison and Secret Snowflakes out of my mind. It was the holiday season, after all. Why should I let Dana ruin that?

"I got the greatest gift for Hanukkah last night," my friend Josh told us. "It's this model of a human skeleton. You have to put it together yourself, like a puzzle. When it's all finished, it will stand three feet tall."

"What are you going to do with it when it's finished?" Chloe asked him.

"Keep it in my room," Josh said. His tone made it clear he didn't think there was any other logical answer.

"So every morning, you're going to wake up to see a human skeleton staring at you?" Chloe asked, not even bothering to hide how creepy she thought that was.

Josh shrugged. "A model human skeleton," he corrected her. "But yeah. I think it's pretty cool."

My friend Marc laughed. "I think it's pretty *Josh*," he said.

I knew exactly what he meant. Josh is a total brain, and the smartest person I know. He's in sixth grade like me, but he's taking seventh grade math. And he's totally into science, too. It didn't really come as any surprise to me that he'd want a skeleton science project as a roommate.

"Well, I found the cutest Christmas present for Bingo," Chloe said, changing the subject back to her two favorite topics — her dog and herself. "It's this headband with antlers attached. He's going to love it!"

I wasn't so sure any dog would want to wear a headband — especially one with antlers on it. But Chloe obviously knew her dog better than I did, so I guess she knew what she was talking about. Then, suddenly, a funny image passed through my mind, and I started to laugh.

"What's so funny?" my friend Liza asked me.

"I was just picturing my pet mice with teeny tiny antlers," I told her.

"That *is* funny," Liza agreed, and she started to laugh, too.

"It never actually occurred to me to buy my mice Christmas gifts, though," I had to admit.

"Lots of people buy gifts for their pets," Chloe told me. "The pet store in the mall was full of candy cane-shaped dog biscuits and pretty gift baskets filled with cat treats."

"I can't believe you've already bought gifts for your dog, and I haven't even bought a gift for my parents yet," Marc admitted. "I have to get on it."

"I'm going shopping this afternoon with Rachel and her mom," I told him. "I just have to get a few little things, though."

"We went shopping last week," my friend Marilyn chimed in.

"But we didn't find anything," her twin sister, Carolyn, added.

"Except your cool new necklace," Marilyn reminded her.

"Oh, yeah," Carolyn recalled. She held up her necklace to give us all a better view.

"It's awesome," I told her. "Those beads are very Christmassy."

"I know," Carolyn said. "But I can wear the necklace all year round."

"You'd better," Marilyn agreed. "It cost you half of the money you'd saved from your allowance."

"That's true," Carolyn said. "But I still have enough to get gifts for you and Mom and Dad."

"I'm not going to do my Christmas shopping until I get to London," Sam announced suddenly.

We all stared at her in surprise.

"You're going to London for Christmas?" I asked her.

Sam nodded. "My mum's been so down in the dumps about being away from family for the holiday that my dad arranged for us to fly over while school's closed. We leave Friday night."

"So you're not going to be spending any of winter break with us?" I asked Sam.

Sam shook her head. "I guess not."

"Bummer," Chloe said. "You're going to miss all the holiday fun."

"People in London have holiday fun, too, Chloe," Liza told her.

That was such a Liza thing to say. She obviously didn't want Sam to feel badly about what she'd be missing while she was away. And Liza's comment had obviously worked, because Sam was smiling. "Of course we do," she said. "My favorite part is on Christmas Eve when we pop the crackers."

"When you what the *what?*" Marilyn and Carolyn asked at the exact same time.

Sam giggled. "Pop the crackers," she explained. "A cracker is a fancy, decorated cardboard tube that you pull from both ends. When it pops open, you find a toy and a paper crown inside. Then everyone has to wear the crown all through dinner. You should see my grandfather sitting there with a paper crown on his big, bald head. It's hilarious."

I just sat there, listening as Sam told us all about what Christmas with her family in England was like. She sounded really happy talking about it. I was glad for her. Really. But I was also bummed for me. I'd been looking forward to spending my first middle school break with *all* of my middle school friends. Now I found out Sam wasn't going to be here.

This day definitely wasn't turning out quite as I'd expected. First I'd gotten Dana as a Secret Snowflake, and now this. Things weren't turning out too Christmassy for me. I sighed and looked out the cafeteria windows.

That little glance toward the world outside of my school was all it took to cheer me up. I could see a few snowflakes starting to fall. They were beautiful: white and cheerful as they danced their way from the clouds to the ground. The snowflakes were just so Christmassy! They brought a real smile to my face. I was going to have to deal with Dana Harrison, and I would miss Sam. Those things were less than perfect, for sure. But Christmas was coming. And nothing could ruin that. Nothing at all.

Chapter
TWO

THE MALL was really crowded by the time Rachel and I got there. Her mom had spent at least half an hour driving around the parking lot looking for a free space. And when we got inside, it really seemed like a sea of people had invaded the mall. I've never seen it that busy before. Of course, I'd never been at the mall right before Christmas, either. Up until now, I'd always made my parents a nice card for Christmas. They'd done all the shopping themselves. But now that I was in middle school and was getting a better allowance, I was able to save up some money to *buy* my parents a gift. I just didn't know what that gift was going to be yet.

My parents' gift wasn't the only one I was clueless about. There were also Dana's three gifts for me to think about, and I knew those were going to be even tougher to come up with than the one for my parents. I'd been racking my brain about them all day, and I still hadn't come up with a single idea for what to make for Dana.

"So, um, Rach," I said, hoping to probe her for some thoughts on what to give a privileged Pop with a bad attitude. "Are you having fun with this whole Secret Snowflake thing?'

Rachel nodded. "Sure. Mine's easy. I got Zachary Sheffield. He's obsessed with hockey. So tonight I'm going to glue pictures of famous hockey players to cardboard. Then he can put them up in his room like posters."

"You weren't supposed to tell anyone who you got as a Secret Snowflake," I reminded her.

Rachel shrugged. "It's okay," she said. "We're not in the same class or anything. And besides, I know you won't tell. Who'd you get?"

I sighed heavily. "Dana Harrison."

"Wow, that really stinks," Rachel told me.

Rachel's mother looked at us. "Why does having Dana Harrison stink?" she asked. "I would think getting someone you girls went all through elementary school with would make things easier. You know her so well. It should be easy to come up with what gifts she would like."

Rachel and I glanced at each other. We weren't

quite sure what to say to that. There's no easy way to explain the middle school popularity food chain to adults. They never seemed to understand.

"Dana's changed a lot since elementary school," Rachel told her mother.

I nodded. "Definitely. And we don't hang around together anymore. So I'm not sure what to make for her."

"Well, what would you like someone to make for you?" Rachel's mom asked me. "I'm sure Dana would like something similar. How different can you girls be, really?"

A whole lot different, I thought to myself. But I didn't say that, of course. Instead I just nodded my head and pretended to agree with her.

"Hey, Mom, can we get a snack before we start shopping?" Rachel asked her mother.

"Definitely," Rachel's mom answered. "I think we could all use an energy boost to make our way through these crowds. Do you girls want a hamburger or something?"

"I love hamburgers," Rachel said. A big smile began to form on her face. "In fact, did you hear the one about the hamburger who went on trial for robbery?"

"No," her mom replied. "What happened?"

"He was found guilty as *charred*," Rachel answered. Then she burst out laughing.

Her mother laughed pretty hard, too. Apparently a love of really bad jokes runs in Rachel's family.

Rachel's mom's words about Dana were stuck in my head all afternoon. And when I got home that evening (with a really pretty Christmas candle that I'd purchased for my mom and dad), I tried to think of a gift that I would want that would also make Dana happy. But nothing was coming to mind. I was definitely going to need a little help with this.

So I did what I always did when I had a middle school problem. I logged on to my favorite website, middleschoolsurvival.com, and typed the words *handmade gifts* into the search box. As the search engine worked its magic, I began to relax. Middleschoolsurvival.com had never let me down before. There was no reason it wouldn't be able to solve this dilemma for me now.

Sure enough, a moment later, a whole list of crafty gift ideas popped up on the screen. I scrolled down for a while, searching for just the right idea. It turned out to be number three on the list.

Christmas Hair Clips

Do want to add some sparkle to your hair this holiday season? These hair clips will do the trick, and you don't even have to ask Santa for them. You can make them all by yourself.

HERE'S WHAT YOU NEED:
Hair clips (the kind that are round or triangular and snap open and closed), brightly colored nail polish, clear nail polish, and craft glitter.

HERE'S WHAT YOU DO:
1. Paint the hair clips with brightly colored nail polish.
2. Sprinkle the glitter over the nail polish while it is still wet. Allow the polish and glitter to dry.
3. Paint a clear coat of nail polish over the colored polish. Allow the polish to dry.

I just happened to have a whole package of brand-new clips in my top drawer. A little while ago I had made the mistake of cutting my own bangs, and now I was trying to grow them out. That meant that lately I wore a lot of hair clips. I also *lost* a lot of hair clips. So my mom tended to pick up new packages of them whenever they were on sale. I decided she wouldn't mind if I used one or two of the new ones to make Dana's first Secret Snowflake gift.

I was feeling pretty good about things as I headed into the bathroom to find some really colorful nail polish. Dana was going to love her Secret Snowflake gift. I was sure of it.

Unfortunately, I wasn't feeling quite so sure the next morning as I walked down the C wing of our middle school on my way to Dana's locker. I'd lost a bit of my confidence on the bus ride over to school. What if Dana thought my gift was totally lame? She was sure to tell everyone how stupid her present was. And then on Friday, when we all revealed ourselves to our Secret Snowflakes, everyone would know I was the geekiest gift giver in the entire sixth grade.

Still, I had to give the clips to Dana. Otherwise she would think that her Secret Snowflake had forgotten her. That was too mean of a thing to do, even to Dana. So, after making sure no one was around to see me, I slipped the glittery clips into the Secret Snowflake envelope Dana had taped to the front of her locker. Then I ran away as fast as I could.

I obviously wasn't the only Secret Snowflake who'd been busy that morning. By the time I reached my locker, someone had placed a gift in the envelope I'd taped to the front. I pulled it out and hurried to unwrap the gift.

"Wow!" I exclaimed as I saw what was inside. My Secret Snowflake had printed out ten pictures of cute little white mice. Each picture was different, but they were all printed on white note cards.

Just then Liza came up behind me. She was wearing the coolest earrings. They were made from tiny red Christmas tree lightbulbs.

"Awesome earrings," I told her.

"Thanks," Liza said. "They light up, too." She pushed a button on the side of one of the earrings, and it started to blink.

"Wow!" I exclaimed. "I wonder how that works."

"Teeny-tiny batteries," Liza explained.

"Are they heavy?" I wondered.

Liza shook her head. "Not at all," she told me. Then she glanced down at the box of cards in my hands.

"Is that your Secret Snowflake gift?" she asked me.

I nodded. "They're note cards," I told her. "Aren't they adorable?"

Liza looked at the collection of cards in my hands. "Whoever gave you those knows you pretty well," she said.

"Definitely," I agreed. "Do seventh graders do Secret Snowflake?"

Liza shook her head. "Nope. Just sixth graders. The seventh graders are having holiday parties in our English classes this year. Everybody has to bring in a snack."

"What are you going to bring in?" I asked.

Liza shrugged. "I don't know. I'm not much of a cook. I figured I'd just go on middleschoolsurvival. com and find a recipe."

"Sounds like a good idea," I told her.

"Do you think the person you gave your gift to will like it as much as you like the note cards?" Liza asked me.

"I hope so," I replied. And I meant it. The last thing I needed was Dana thinking her gift was lousy. If that happened, I'd never live it down when our identities were revealed.

There was only one way I could find out what Dana thought. I would have to listen carefully in English class to see if she said anything about her gift.

Actually, Dana didn't have to say a word. Her hair said it all. She was wearing both clips on the right side of her head. I had to admit they looked really cool.

"I think I'm starting a new trend," I overheard Dana telling Addie.

"Those do look great in your hair," Addie agreed. "But I don't know about a trend. I don't think that by tomorrow everyone will be wearing glittery hair clips."

I rolled my eyes. That was such an Addie thing to say. In her mind she was the only person who could start fashion trends at Joyce Kilmer Middle School.

"Well, I think they're cool," Dana said. "And whoever gave them to me has a definite sense of style." She shot Addie a knowing smile.

Addie shrugged. "They're nice enough," she said. "I got a package of candy kisses wrapped in green and red foil. I guess whoever gave them to me thought I was sweet."

That made me laugh inside. I doubted anyone actually thought Addie Wilson was sweet. Fashionable, maybe. Popular, definitely. But sweet? Never!

I looked around the room, trying to figure out who had given me my gift. But no one was giving me any signs or clues. Of course, Chloe and Sam hadn't arrived yet. And I remembered what Liza had said about the person who had made the cards knowing me really well.

"So, what'd you get, mate?" Sam asked me a moment later as she plopped down at the desk beside mine.

Okay, that meant Sam wasn't my Secret Snowflake. If she were, she'd have already known what I'd gotten. "Note cards," I told her. "Really cute ones."

"I got this pin," Sam told me.

I looked at the handmade clay pin on Sam's blazer. It was shaped like a little Christmas tree. It was cute, but not really Sam's taste. I figured she was only wearing it so she wouldn't hurt her Secret Snowflake's feelings.

"What'd you get, Chloe?" I asked as Chloe walked into the classroom.

"Earrings," Chloe said. She held up two small homemade beaded hoops. "Which would be great, if I had pierced ears."

I sighed. It was clear whoever Chloe's and Sam's Secret Snowflake gift givers were, they didn't know too much about my friends. I felt badly for them. Especially since my Secret Snowflake seemed to know me really well.

"Okay, class, settle down," Ms. Jaffe said. "I know you're all really excited about your first Secret Snowflake gifts, but we've got a lot of actual English to work on today. So put away your presents, and let's get to it."

There was a loud grumble in the classroom. No one was in the mood to work, but who could blame us? With only three days to go until the break, our brains were already on vacation. All anyone could think about was all the fun and excitement coming up. I couldn't wait to find out what plans my friends and I were going to come up with for our winter break.

Chapter
THREE

THAT NIGHT, as I sat in my bedroom doing my math homework (why do teachers give homework three days before vacation, anyway?), my cell phone rang. It was Chloe.

"Hey, Chlo," I said as I answered the call.

"Hey, Jenny, what are you up to?" she asked me.

"Math," I groaned. "But I'm going to give up soon and start making my Secret Snowflake gift for tomorrow."

"Oh," Chloe said. "What are you going to make?"

I laughed. "Nice try, Chloe," I said. "I'm not giving away my identity."

Chloe laughed, too. "Why not? I know you're not my Secret Snowflake. You know me well enough not to get me earrings."

"I'm not telling you whose name I got, Chloe," I said.

"Hey, it was worth a shot," she replied. "I was just curious. Actually, I'm really curious to find out who has *me*. I'd like to introduce myself to him or her. It's clear my Secret Snowflake has never met me."

"The earrings were pretty, though," I said. "I mean, if you were to get your ears pierced."

"True," Chloe agreed. "Maybe someday. I'm just not all that into having holes punched into my head."

"It doesn't hurt that much," I told her. "It really just stings for a second. And then it's all over."

"Whatever," Chloe said. She was obviously eager to change the subject. "So have you thought about what you're going to wear to Marc's party?"

That caught me completely off guard. I had no idea what Chloe was talking about. "What party?" I asked her.

"Marc's New Year's Eve party," Chloe said.

"I didn't know he was having a New Year's Eve party," I replied.

"Didn't you get an invitation?" Chloe asked me.

A knot started to form in the bottom of my stomach. My heart began pounding slightly as well. "N-no," I said softly.

"Of course you did," Chloe said. "He invited a bunch of people. Didn't you check your locker on the way home? Marc taped the invitations to the front of all our lockers right before the end of the day."

Now I felt better. "I didn't stop at my locker before I got on the bus," I told Chloe. "I was cold all day so I already had my coat on."

"That explains it," Chloe said cheerfully. "You'll just pick up your invitation tomorrow when you get to school."

"Yeah," I agreed.

"So what do you think you'll wear to the party?" Chloe asked me.

"I don't know," I said honestly. "I haven't had a chance to think about it. This is the first I've heard about it."

"True," Chloe agreed. "We can talk tomorrow after you get the invitation."

"Sounds good," I said. "Now I've got to hang up, finish these problems, and make my gift."

"What did you say that gift was?" Chloe asked me.

"You don't quit, do you?" I replied.

"I'm nothing if not determined," Chloe agreed. "Talk to you tomorrow."

The next morning, I hurried off the school bus as quickly as possible. I wanted to get Dana's gift into her envelope right away. The quicker I did that, the quicker I could get to my own locker and find my invitation to Marc's party.

But I didn't get very far before I bumped into Marilyn and Carolyn. They were standing in the parking lot, chatting with a couple of seventh graders. But when they saw me, they broke off their conversation and came over to say hi.

"Nice hat," I told Marilyn. She was wearing a really cute rainbow-colored hat. It was made of wool and had a big floppy brim that framed her face perfectly.

"Thanks," Marilyn said. "I saw it in this store in the mall, and I just had to get it."

I laughed. Between Carolyn's necklace (which she was wearing again today) and Marilyn's hat, it didn't seem like the twins were getting a whole lot of Christmas shopping done during their trips to the mall. At least not when it came to getting gifts for other people.

"I wish I didn't have to take my hat off in school," Marilyn continued. "It would be so cool to be able to wear it all day."

But we all knew she couldn't do that. We're not allowed to wear hats in school. It's in the middle school orientation handbook they give everyone when they start sixth grade. And even though I was the only person I knew who had read the handbook from cover to cover, everybody knew about that rule.

But I didn't have time to talk about hats or rules. I had things I had to do. "Listen, you guys, I have to run," I told the twins. "I have to get my Secret Snowflake gift into its envelope before anyone sees me."

Marilyn and Carolyn both nodded. "Okay," Marilyn said cheerfully.

"See you at lunch," Carolyn added.

I took off like a shot and raced down the C wing hallway to Dana's locker. Quickly, I slipped my gift into her envelope and then raced to my locker. I couldn't wait to get my invitation to Marc's party. From what Chloe had said, I knew it was going to be a great time. I'd never been to a New Year's Eve party without my parents before. It sounded so cool.

But when I got to my locker, I didn't see an invitation. The only thing there was my Secret Snowflake envelope. I looked around on the floor to see if maybe the invitation had fallen. But there was nothing there.

I could feel tears starting to burn in my eyes. I

swallowed hard and blinked for a minute. Other kids were starting to filter into the hallway. I didn't want to have to explain to any of them why I was crying. Instead I reached into my Secret Snowflake envelope and pulled out my gift. Then I spent a long time staring at the wrapping and carefully pulling off the paper. As long as I focused on that, I figured nobody would notice how upset I was.

The gift was really nice. My Secret Snowflake had used pipe cleaners and tinsel to make a beautiful shimmery star ornament for my Christmas tree. It looked like it had taken a long time to make. Whoever had picked my name from the hat was spending a lot of time on me. And I was glad, because I'd been spending a lot of time making my gifts, too.

And it was paying off. Dana's locker was pretty far down the hall from mine, but I could still hear her squeal as she opened her gift.

"This is so awesome," she told Addie and Claire. "It's a mirror with a picture of Cody Tucker glued to the back. He's my favorite singer. This gift is so totally me! Whoever my Secret Snowflake is, she's really cool."

I had to laugh despite myself. If Dana only knew who she was calling cool, she'd be really embarrassed. I knew for sure that Dana didn't think I was cool at all.

I sighed heavily. Apparently she wasn't the only one who thought I was too much of a geek to actually hang out with. Marc thought so, too. Here I'd been thinking he was one of my very best friends, and all this time he hadn't liked me at all. At least not enough to invite me to his party.

I slipped into English class just before the bell rang and took the first seat I saw, which was pretty far from where Chloe and Sam were sitting. I didn't want to have to listen to Chloe going on and on about a party I wasn't invited to. I figured there would be plenty of time for that, considering Marc had invited everyone but me. I wasn't ready for that just yet. I wasn't sure I'd ever be ready, but I knew I definitely wasn't right now.

Still, I couldn't avoid Chloe forever, and as we walked out of class, she cornered me.

"So, did you find the invitation?" she asked me.

I shook my head and looked down at the ground. "It wasn't there."

"What do you mean it wasn't there?"

I stared at Chloe with surprise. "Which word didn't you understand?" I snapped at her. Then I stopped myself. That had been really mean. And I wasn't mad at Chloe. I was mad at Marc. "Sorry," I added. "I'm just a little weirded out about not being invited."

"That's ridiculous," Chloe told me. "You have to have been invited. I'll just go ask Marc what happened and . . ."

"No!" I shouted out. Then I blushed slightly as I realized how many people had turned to look at me. "Just leave it alone, Chloe," I said, lowering my voice. "I don't want anyone to ask Marc about this."

"But . . ." Chloe started.

"No buts," I said, interrupting her. "If you're really my friend, you won't say a word about this to anyone."

"Okay," Chloe agreed.

I nodded, hoping that for once, Chloe could keep a secret.

Just then, Sam came out of the classroom. "What are you two talking about?" she asked Chloe and me.

I forced a fake smile. "The Secret Snowflake thing," I lied. "I got a really pretty tree ornament. You want to see it?"

*   *   *

The day only got worse. When I got to the lunch table, everyone was talking about Marc's party.

"Are your folks really going to let us stay at your house until twelve-thirty?" Liza asked him.

Marc nodded. "It's a special night."

"I love New Year's Eve," Marilyn said.

"Me, too," Carolyn agreed.

Chloe chuckled. "There's a shock. Marilyn and Carolyn agree on something."

Everyone laughed at that. Well, everyone but me, anyway. I wasn't in the mood to laugh.

"My dad said he'd order in lots of pizzas for us to eat," Marc said. "And we'll have chips, and my mom said we could toast the New Year with soda poured into champagne glasses."

I glared at Marc. I didn't mind the other kids talking about the party in front of me. After all, other than Chloe, they didn't have any idea that I hadn't been invited to the party. But Marc knew, and he was still going on and on about it. How rude was that?

I wasn't the only one not talking about the party. Sam was also staying out of the conversation. But she didn't look upset. She wasn't going to be part of the New Year's celebration, either, but that was only because she wasn't going to be here.

She was going to be ringing in the New Year with her other friends in London.

But I didn't have any other friends. Up until now I'd spent every New Year's Eve with my parents. The families in my neighborhood always had a New Year's Eve progressive dinner party. Each year the party would start at my house, with my parents serving hors d'oeuvres like spinach pies, goat cheese and mushroom tarts, and cheese and crackers. After that we would all move on to someone else's house for salad, and another house for the main meal. Usually Addie's family served the dessert.

The New Year's Eve progressive dinner could actually be a lot of fun. Or at least it had been fun when I was in elementary school. But this year I knew it wouldn't be any fun at all. Even if Addie was at the progressive dinner (which I doubted; the Pops were probably having their own party), she wouldn't want to hang around with me. So I'd be all by myself the whole night, while everyone else in the entire world was having a great time with their friends.

Suddenly I stood up and began to walk my tray over to the garbage.

"Jenny, where are you going?" Liza asked me.

I looked pointedly at Marc, and bit my lower lip to keep from crying. "To the library to study," I told Liza. "I've lost my appetite."

Marc's party was on my mind all day long. I tried to think of something I could have said or done that would have made him mad at me. But there was nothing I could think of. We'd been getting along just fine. Until now.

Maybe Marc thought I didn't like parties. Or maybe he thought I acted weird at parties, and that was why he didn't want me there. But I didn't think I acted strangely at all. In fact, I thought I seemed really comfortable hanging out with my friends. And my friends would definitely be at Marc's party.

There was only one way for me to figure out if other people didn't see me as the party type. I would have to log on to my favorite website and find a quiz that would answer the question for me. So I raced over to my computer and typed in www.middleschoolsurvival.com. Instantly, the site appeared on the screen. I scanned the quizzes until I found exactly what I was looking for.

Who's a Party Animal?

Do you have a roaring good time whenever you're in a social situation? Or do you keep to yourself? If you want to find out whether or not you're the life of the party, we invite you to take this quiz.

1. You hear there's a party happening on Friday night, but you don't really know the host. What do you do?

A. Find a friend who's been invited and ask to tag along.

B. Make other plans. If you're not invited, you're not invited.

C. Just show up. What's one more guest?

Wow! Talk about a question that went right to the heart of the matter. I had already heard about a party that I hadn't been invited to. Of course I knew the host of this party, but the basic gist of the question was the same. I knew my answer couldn't be A. After all, I knew a lot of people who were invited to Marc's party, and I hadn't asked any of them if I could tag along. I also knew that I wasn't the kind of person to crash a party she wasn't invited to. Which meant C was also out of the question. So I clicked "B" and waited for the next question to appear on the screen.

2. The party is loud and crowded with people. Who do you find yourself talking to?

A. Just people I know from school.

B. My friends and the people they've introduced me to.

C. Whoever happens to be dancing near me.

I thought back to all the dances and parties I'd been to since I started middle school. I'm pretty friendly, and I talk to a lot of people. But I'm rarely – if ever – away from my friends at a party. Since Liza, Marc, and the twins are all seventh graders, they know a whole lot more people at the school than I do. And whenever they're talking to other seventh graders they know, they always include me in the conversation. So I figured my answer had to be B. I clicked the mouse and then waited for the next question.

3. Where do you hang out when you're at a party?

A. All over the place — I like to circulate.

B. Right near the snacks.

C. On the dance floor.

That one was easy. My answer was definitely A. When I'm at a party, I want to do it all — dance, talk to my friends, and eat. Especially if the snacks are good. Which I was pretty sure they would be at Marc's house.

I sighed heavily and tried to push all the thoughts of Marc's party out of my head. I was supposed to be focusing on the quiz questions. However, since I was taking the quiz because of Marc's party, that wasn't exactly an easy task. Still, the next question had already popped up on the screen.

4. **When you are at a party, do you go out of your way to introduce yourself to someone you have never met before?**

A. I don't usually. I'm kind of shy around new people.

B. Always. It's a lot of fun to meet new people.

C. Sometimes, especially if I don't know too many people at the party.

Hmm. That question wasn't as easy. I know how important it is to introduce yourself to new people, because I met my new crowd of friends when Chloe introduced herself to me. But I'm not Chloe, and I find it hard to just go up to people and say, "Hi! I'm

Jenny." I usually wait to be introduced. So I figured my answer had to be A.

5. What's your favorite party-time activity?

A. Watching TV
B. Eating snacks
C. Playing games

I knew I could cross A off the list right away. I rarely watch TV at a party. I can do that by myself at home. So that left eating snacks and playing games. I like both of them equally. But since you usually need a lot of people to play games, and that meant that was a special party activity I couldn't do at home (especially since I'm an only child), I clicked my mouse over the letter C, and waited to see what popped up next on my computer screen.

Use this chart to add up your score.

1. A. 2 points   B. 1 point   C. 3 points
2. A. 1 point   B. 2 points   C. 3 points
3. A. 3 points   B. 1 point   C. 2 points
4. A. 1 point   B. 3 points   C. 2 points
5. A. 1 point   B. 2 points   C. 3 points

So Are You a Party Animal?

5-8 points: When it comes to group gatherings, you tend to be skittish and shy. And while it's okay to prefer the company of a few close friends over the party scene, you might want to venture out a bit. You may discover that the more you talk to new people, the easier it becomes.

9-12 points: When it comes to parties, you know how to have a good time, but you're not the kind of girl to go out of control. You're equally comfortable in a large or small setting. Congrats to you — you've found the perfect party balance.

13-15 points: Look up party animal in the dictionary, and there's a good chance your photo will be there! You love a good celebration, and no matter what the party, you're right there in the middle of it. Just make sure you don't get too wild. Making the scene is fun — making a scene can be a social disaster.

It was just as I'd suspected. With ten points, I was the perfect party guest. I didn't hang by the wall, staring at everyone and making them feel uncomfortable, and I didn't make myself the complete center of attention. I was proud of my score. It's nice to know you're the kind of person most people would want at their party. But the answer also really confused me. If I was such a perfect party guest, then why didn't Marc want me at his party?

Just then my phone rang. The call was coming from Marilyn and Carolyn's landline. "Hello," I said as I answered my cell phone.

"Hi, Jenny," one of the twins (I wasn't sure which) said.

"Hi, Jenny," the other twin echoed.

I shook my head. It was hard enough to tell Marilyn and Carolyn apart when you were with them in person. On the phone, it was absolutely impossible. "Hi, guys," I replied.

"We're having a party," one of the twins told me.

"On Christmas Eve," her sister added.

"It's a tree trimming," they said together.

"That sounds fun," I told them.

"So you'll come?" one of the twins asked.

"You bet!" I exclaimed happily.

"Great!" the twins cheered.

"It's going to be awesome," one of them told me.

"First we'll trim the tree, and then we're all going to go caroling," the other said.

"I hope it's snowing," I chimed in. "Caroling in the snow is a lot of fun."

As the twins and I spoke more about their Christmas Eve tree-trimming party, a big smile formed on my face. Maybe Marc didn't want me coming to a party at his house, but Marilyn and Carolyn did. Apparently, I wasn't a *total* loser in the party department after all.

Chapter
FOUR

I WASN'T A LOSER in the gift-giving department, either. As I rode the bus to school the next morning, I was feeling really confident about the present I'd made for Dana the night before. It was perfect for her. And even though today was the day we were revealing our true identities to the people we'd been giving gifts to, I knew she wouldn't be able to deny that my gifts had been really cool.

"Do you have your Secret Snowflake gift?" I asked my friend Felicia as she sat down next to me on the bus.

"Oh, yeah," she said. "It was really hard for me to do the whole Secret Snowflake thing. I got Charlie Feld and I hardly know him at all."

"He's the kid who's obsessed with video games, right?" I asked her.

Felicia nodded. "Try coming up with a craft for that," she said. "It's not like he's an interesting boy, like Josh or something."

I smiled. Josh and Felicia are girlfriend and boy-friend, and as far as Felicia is concerned, Josh is the perfect guy.

"So who'd you get for Secret Snowflake?" Felicia asked me.

I started to answer her, and then caught a glimpse of Addie Wilson, who was sitting on the other side of the bus, a few rows behind us. Addie was sitting all by herself, as usual. She was the only Pop on our bus, which meant she never shared her seat with anyone, and no one ever attempted to sit next to her. It's kind of an unwritten rule in middle school that Pops never sit with non-Pops.

I could tell Addie was listening to what Felicia and I were saying, even though she was pretending not to. And I definitely didn't want her to be the one to tell Dana that I'd been the one to give her gifts. So I just smiled mysteriously at Felicia and said, "I'm not telling."

"Oh, come on," she said. "I told *you*."

That was true. But I still didn't want to tell her. So I changed the subject. "Are you bringing an ornament to the twins' house on Christmas Eve?" I asked her.

Felicia nodded. "I'm not sure if I'm going to make one or buy one, though."

"I think I'm probably going to make an ornament for them," I told her. "That way I can be sure I've gotten them one they don't already have."

"That's a good idea," Felicia said. "I just don't know if I'll have time between now and Christmas Eve."

Just then, the bus pulled into the school parking lot. As Felicia and I got off the bus, Rachel was there waiting for us.

"Just the people I was hoping to see," Rachel said. "I need a favor from you guys."

"What's up?" I asked her.

"My cousin Maddie is coming to visit for the vacation," Rachel explained. "She lives in California, and my dad and I are picking her up at the airport after school today. I was hoping you guys could come with us."

"I'll ask my mom," I told her. "But since it's Friday, and vacation starts right after school, I can't imagine she'll say no."

"Same here," Felicia assured her. "What time does her flight get in?"

"Eight o'clock," Rachel said.

"What's your cousin like?" I asked.

Rachel smiled. "She's cool. Very big city, Los Angeles. You really have to meet her in person."

"Okay," I said. "I guess we'll do that tonight."

"Thanks so much, you guys," Rachel said. "It'll make Maddie so happy to have two new friends. She's going to be really grateful."

I hoped Dana would be just as grateful for the gift I'd slipped into her Secret Snowflake envelope before English class. I sat there with my fingers crossed as she walked into the classroom a few minutes before class began.

"Okay, Addie, now I know you're my Secret Snowflake," she said. "No one else would know that I'd tried on strawberry lip gloss at the mall last week." She proceeded to rub a generous amount of the homemade gloss I'd made for her on her lips. "This stuff tastes like strawberry, too. How'd you make it?"

"I swear to you, Dana, I'm not your Secret Snowflake," Addie said with an exasperated sigh. "I told you that last night."

"But you have to be," Dana insisted loudly. "None of the losers in here would ever have been able to come up with the kinds of gifts I got. Only a truly cool person would have done that."

I smiled so wide I thought my jaw would crack open. I couldn't hold it in another minute. And besides, it was the day we were going to reveal ourselves, anyway. So I just shouted out, "Addie wasn't your Secret Snowflake, Dana. I was."

Dana's eyes opened wide. She stared at me for a minute, and then made a face. She raced up to Ms. Jaffe's desk and grabbed a tissue. Then she wiped all the gloss from her lips.

"I should have known," Dana told me. "This stuff tastes gross. Which makes sense since you're pretty gross yourself."

I shook my head in disbelief. Did Dana think I was a complete idiot? The entire class had already heard her say what a great gift the lip gloss was. Nothing she said now was going to change that.

I was actually proud of myself. Despite Dana's protests, I knew she had liked the gifts. I'd managed to make her happy with things that I would have liked to receive myself. I figured that might be what was upsetting Dana so much. Based on her reaction to the gifts, it was clear that the Pops and the non-Pops weren't that different. We all liked pretty much the same kinds of things. That idea must have made her crazy.

I was so caught up in my thoughts about Dana that I'd almost forgotten to open my own gift. Quickly, I tore open the wrapping paper and pulled out a bracelet made from red, white, and blue twisted wires.

"Awesome!" I exclaimed. "This is the best gift I've gotten yet."

"I'm so glad you like it," Sam said with a smile. "It took me a really long time to make it."

"It was you!" I exclaimed happily. "I knew it had to be one of my friends."

"Of course it was me," she said. "Who else could it have been?"

"It was either you or Chloe," I told her. "No one else here knows how much I love my mice." I paused for a minute. "Except Addie, I guess. But she never would have put as much time into my gifts as you did."

"Okay," Chloe said suddenly. "This is more like it."

"What did you get?" I asked her.

Chloe held up a keychain. It had a whistle attached to it. "I can use this when I'm playing outside with Bingo. Instead of calling for him, I can whistle for him." She put the whistle to her mouth and blew. The whistle was pretty shrill, and really loud.

Unfortunately, Ms. Jaffe walked right into the classroom just as Chloe was blowing her whistle.

"Chloe!" our teacher exclaimed. "What are you doing?"

"Sorry, Ms. Jaffe," Chloe replied sheepishly. "I was just testing out my Secret Snowflake gift."

I expected Ms. Jaffe to be angry with Chloe for blowing a whistle in class, but she wasn't. Instead she laughed. "Well, I guess this is as good a time as any for you to reveal yourselves to the person you've been giving gifts to this week."

I was kind of amazed that Ms. Jaffe had been so cool about Chloe and the whistle. But I guess even teachers find it hard to be angry on the day before vacation.

English class went really fast that day — probably because we didn't do any school work. We just spent the time talking about our gifts with our friends. It turned out Kip Parker had given Chloe her gifts. I wasn't really surprised. I kind of figured her Secret Snowflake had to be a boy, because boys never know what to get a girl. Sam's presents had been from Emily Cooper, a really quiet, but sweet, girl who always sat in the front row in class.

"That lip gloss you gave Dana was too good of a gift for her," Chloe whispered to me a few minutes later. She knew she couldn't say it out loud. Even on the day before vacation, that was the kind of comment that a teacher would never stand for.

"She's too evil to get such a nice gift," Sam agreed. "How did you make that, anyway?"

"I found the instructions on middleschoolsurvival. com," I told her. "I think I might actually have the printout with me. I shoved it in my backpack with some other papers that were on my desk." I opened my pack and searched through my stuff. "Yeah, here it is," I said, handing the piece of paper to Sam.

Fresh and Fruity Homemade Lip Gloss

This homemade makeup recipe will give your lips a glamorous, glossy look. Everything you need for this fashion-forward fruity lip gloss can be found right in your kitchen!

YOU WILL NEED:
2 tablespoons solid shortening, 1 tablespoon fruit-flavored powdered drink mix (in the color of your choice), 1 clean, small container

HERE'S WHAT YOU DO:

1. Combine the shortening and the powdered drink mix in a microwave–safe bowl. Mix until smooth.

2. Place the shortening and drink mix combination in the microwave and cook on high for 30 seconds or until the mix has become a liquid.

3. Carefully pour the liquid mix into a clean, small container. Ask an adult for help, as the liquid will be hot.

4. Place the container in the refrigerator for 30 minutes or until firm.

"I'm going to mix up a batch of this with grape powdered drink mix," Sam said. "How cool would it be to have purple lip gloss?"

"Pretty cool," I said. "And also pretty you."

"That's the truth," Chloe agreed. "I don't know anyone else who would look perfectly normal with purple lips."

I looked at the green streak going down the right side of Sam's hair, and the red streak going down the left side. No one else in school had streaked their hair for Christmas. Sam really was the only person who could pull off the purple lip gloss thing.

"Of course, I'll have to wait until I get home after vacation to make it," Sam told us. "I'm going right to the airport from school today."

"Oh wow, that's right," I said, suddenly feeling really bummed out. "You're leaving for England."

Sam gave me a smile. "But not until the end of the day, chum. We still have two classes and lunch together."

Lunch. Grrrr. Not even Sam could make that better for me. The very first person I saw when I arrived in the cafeteria was Marc. He was already sitting at our lunch table, eating his meatball sub.

I had no desire to hurry up and share the table with Marc, so I took my time getting my lunch, looking over everything in the sandwich line (even though they always had the same lunch meats, tuna salad, and cheese every day). And I also considered forgetting lunch all together and just going to the library. But I stopped myself. There was no way I was going to let Marc do that to me. He could choose not to invite me to his party, but he wasn't going to disinvite me from my own lunch table. So I got into the hot-lunch line and picked up my meatball sub and salad. By the time my tray was full, Liza, Chloe, Josh, and the twins were all at our table already.

"I think the no-hat rule is idiotic," Marilyn was saying as I put my tray on the table and took a seat. "My new hat matches this blouse perfectly. It would complete my look."

Carolyn fingered her necklace. She was obviously glad that there was no rule that prevented her from wearing *her* Christmas gift to herself. "I agree with you," she told Marilyn. "This school doesn't leave us any room for originality of style."

"Unless, of course, you're a Pop," I pointed out.

Chloe shook her head. "They may have a style," she said, "but there's no originality there."

I looked over at the Pops' table. Addie, Claire, Dana, Maya, and Sabrina were each wearing either a green or a red sweater, and tight "skinny" jeans. Chloe was right, they were stylish, but not at all original.

Chloe, on the other hand, was very original. At the moment, she was wearing a T-shirt that read *But, Santa, I can explain* . . . It was hilarious, and totally Chloe. *She* was an original.

"Speaking of originality, wait until you guys see the way we decorated our house for Christmas this year," Marc piped up.

Everyone turned their attention over to him. Everyone but me, that is. There was no way I was going to even look over in his direction. I didn't care what his Christmas decorations were like. It wasn't like I was ever going to be invited over to his house to see them.

"We've got a Santa sleigh that actually moves back and forth on a track sitting right on our front lawn," Marc said. "And all of our lights are green and red."

"Your house is nice," Chloe complimented him. "But ours is definitely the coolest house on the block. We've got white lights in all of our trees, and a huge blow-up Frosty the Snowman on the lawn. And we sprayed fake snow on all our windows. Our house looks just like the North Pole."

"The North Pole without Santa Claus," Marc pointed out.

"We don't need plastic reindeer, anyway," Chloe told Marc. "All I have to do is put Bingo's reindeer headband on him and let him run around our yard. Then we have a real, live reindeer dog!"

Marc wasn't about to agree with that. "Our house is much more Christmassy," he insisted.

"We'll be the judge of that," Josh said. "You guys live right next door to each other. When we come over for the New Year's Eve party, we'll look at both houses, and we'll make the final determination."

That was it. Just the mention of Marc's party and I got a sick, sinking feeling in my stomach. That feeling must have shown up on my face, because Chloe looked at me strangely. Then she turned her attention over to Marc, and started to say something. I knew she was going to ask him about my invitation, right here, in front of all of our friends. And I couldn't think of anything more embarrassing. So I stopped her before she could say a word.

"Rachel's cousin Maddie is flying in from Los Angeles tonight," I announced, changing the subject as quickly as possible. "She's never been in a cold climate for Christmas. It should be pretty exciting for her."

"It would be nice if it snowed on Christmas," Liza said. "A white Christmas is always the best."

"I bet Rachel's cousin would love that," I said.

"I know I would," Marilyn agreed. "My hat would keep me warm."

"You and that hat," Carolyn teased. "I bet you wish you could staple it to your head."

We all laughed at that. It was clear everyone was in a good mood today. And I was starting to feel that way again. At least no one was talking about the New Year's Eve party anymore. We were all focused on other things. And that definitely made me happier.

Chapter
FIVE

MARC'S PARTY was the last thing on my mind as I raced through the airport that evening with Rachel's family and Felicia. The only thought going through my mind was *hurry*. Maybe that was because that was what Rachel's mother kept saying over and over to us. There had been a lot of traffic on the way to airport, and we were late getting there. Maddie's plane had already landed.

"That poor kid," Rachel's mother said as we raced over to the luggage pick-up area. "She's probably standing there all alone."

"No she's not," Rachel's dad assured her. "She'll have a flight attendant there with her. When kids fly alone there's always a flight attendant that takes care of them until an adult picks them up."

I thought it was really amazing that Rachel's cousin had flown all the way from California on her own. The few times I'd been on a plane, I'd gone with both of my parents. I couldn't imagine sitting all by myself for six hours on an airplane full of strangers. I figured Maddie must be really brave.

"There she is!" Rachel's mom shouted out. "Maddie! Maddie! We're here!"

A girl with long, straight brown hair turned around and looked in our direction. She looked a little like Rachel, only taller, and slightly tanned. "Hi, Aunt Grace," she said with a weary grin as we came closer. "Actually people call me Madison now."

"Oh," Rachel's mom said. "I'm sorry. Madison is much more grownup sounding."

Madison didn't answer her. She just stood there, looking around.

"So sorry we're late," Rachel's father told the flight attendant. He pulled out his wallet and showed her his driver's license. I guess the airline needed some proof that he and Rachel's mom were really the people who were supposed to pick up Maddie — I mean *Madison* — at the airport.

"Let's get your luggage," Rachel's dad said to Madison as the flight attendant walked away.

"Well, these two pieces are mine," Madison said, pointing to two large matching brown leather suitcases. "The third one hasn't come down yet."

"What does it look like?" Rachel asked her cousin.

Madison rolled her eyes. "Exactly like those two, Rachel. It's a set."

Felicia shot me a look. I understood what she meant. Madison sounded kind of mean. And I noticed she hadn't even said hello to Rachel or her dad yet. But maybe she was just tired after such a long flight.

"Do I know you two?" Madison asked, looking over at Felicia and me.

"Oh, these are my friends Felicia and Jenny," Rachel introduced us. "I brought them so you could meet them now. That way you'll at least know the three of us when we do things with my friends over the break."

"Hi, Madison," I said, using the name she wanted to be called by, and trying to sound as friendly as I could.

"Hi," Felicia echoed.

Madison didn't say hi back. In fact, she just shrugged and turned her attention back to the luggage that was being unloaded. "I hope they didn't lose my third bag. It has my favorite jeans in it."

"I'm sure it's here," Rachel's dad assured her.

"There are still plenty of pieces of luggage coming down."

"Three suitcases. Wow," Felicia remarked. "How long are you staying, anyway?"

"Until the day after New Year's," Madison told her. "I wanted to bring more clothes, of course, but my mother wouldn't let me. She said I could always do laundry if I needed to. Can you imagine that? Doing laundry on vacation?"

I wasn't quite sure how to answer that. It wasn't like she was going to be spending vacation in a hotel or anything. She was going to Rachel's house. And there was a washing machine there. I actually thought Madison's mother was right. But I figured Madison wasn't in the mood to hear that right now.

Eventually her third suitcase appeared, and Rachel's dad pulled it off the conveyer belt for her. As soon as he did, Madison began to head for the door, leaving her suitcases behind her. Rachel's dad grabbed one and began pulling it by the handle toward the door. Rachel's mom grabbed the second one, and Rachel took the third. Luckily they all had wheels. Those suitcases looked way too heavy to carry very far.

"Do you believe her?" Felicia whispered to me as we followed Rachel's family to the parking lot. "What does she think Rachel is, her slave?"

"Rachel said Madison was really cool," I reminded her.

"I don't think so," Felicia said. "She's a total snob."

I have to admit I agreed with Felicia. But I was trying hard not to be too judgmental. After all, I'd only known Madison for five minutes.

But the forty-five-minute drive back to Rachel's house in the minivan didn't do a whole lot to change my mind about Madison. She didn't have one nice thing to say the whole time.

"It's weird to see the trees without any leaves," she mentioned as she looked out the car window. "Back home everything is so green. And palm trees don't lose their fronds or anything. Home is so alive. Everything here is dead."

"The trees might not have leaves, but they look beautiful with the icicles hanging from them," Rachel told her. "Just like you see in all those Christmas movies."

"We're going to have a real Christmas," Rachel's dad said.

"We have Christmas in Los Angeles, too, Uncle Frank," Madison told him. "It's just nice and warm. We're not all bundled up in coats and hats and stuff."

The way Madison said "coats and hats" she made it sound like they were the most awful things in the world.

"I like your coat, Madison," Rachel's mother complimented her. "It looks very warm."

"I got it when we went skiing last year," Madison replied. She turned to Rachel, Felicia, and me. "We have snow in California, too. It's in the north. We have pretty much everything in California."

"I've seen the commercials," Felicia said. I could tell by the tone in her voice that she was getting pretty annoyed with Madison. Not that I blamed her. I was getting annoyed, too. In fact, I was really glad when Rachel's dad pulled the minivan up in front of my house a few minutes later.

"First stop, Jenny's house," Rachel's dad called out, sounding a lot like a train conductor. Rachel, Felicia, and I all laughed. Madison yawned.

"I'll see you guys tomorrow," I said. "We're going skating, right?"

"Yup," Rachel said. "We're meeting everyone else at the rink at eleven."

"Do you skate, Madison?" I asked her as I climbed out of the van.

Madison shrugged. "I've never done it. But it doesn't look that hard."

I knew Madison was wrong. I'd taken more than a few skating lessons, and I still fell plenty. But I didn't bother to tell her that. I figured she'd learn how tough ice-skating was all on her own.

"Thanks again for coming, Jenny," Rachel's mom said.

"No problem," I replied. "It was really fun."

As I walked up the path to my house, I touched my hand to my nose. I had to make sure it wasn't growing like Pinocchio's, because I had just told a whopper of a lie. Meeting Madison had been *anything* but fun.

A good night's sleep didn't do much to change Madison. By the time Felicia's mom had dropped us off at the skating rink on Saturday morning, I was pretty sure Rachel was ready to put her cousin on the next plane back to Los Angeles. And if she wasn't, Felicia and I were.

"It's so cold in your house, Rachel," Madison complained as we got our rental skates. "And now it's cold in here. Aren't you sick of being cold all the time?"

"It's winter, and this is an ice-skating rink," Rachel reminded her. "It's supposed to be cold."

"I spent last Christmas in Acapulco with my parents," Madison said. "We were on the beach the whole time — when we weren't breaking piñatas with sticks at the hotel. Now *that's* fun."

The way she said that, I could tell she meant that *this* wasn't fun. "If you wanted to go somewhere warm for the holidays, why are you here?" I asked her.

I hadn't meant it to sound mean. It was just a question. And it seemed like a pretty logical one, at least to me. But something I had said must have hit a nerve with Madison because I could swear I saw her tear up a little bit, and she was suddenly really quiet. But a moment later, her eyes dried up and she went right back to being her cranky self.

"My parents thought I should have an old-fashioned Christmas," she said as she looked around at the happy skaters circling the rink. "And this town is definitely old-fashioned."

Rachel looked at me helplessly. I could tell she felt really badly about how Madison was acting.

And she seemed a little surprised, too. Apparently, her cousin had changed a lot since she'd last seen her. The Madison Felicia and I had met was definitely not someone you'd be excited to have stay at your house or meet your friends.

I took one look at Felicia's face, and I knew there was about to be trouble. I couldn't let an argument break out between the two of them. So I grabbed Felicia by the hand and said, "Look, there's Liza and the twins. Let's go skate with them."

And with that, she and I took off onto the ice. I felt kind of bad about leaving Rachel all alone with her cousin, but it was the only thing I could think of to do.

"Is that Rachel's cousin?" Liza asked me as Felicia and I skated over to where she, Marilyn, and Carolyn were.

I nodded. "Her name's Madison."

"It should be *Brat*ison," Felicia said. "She's so totally spoiled. She came here with three suitcases for a ten-day vacation."

"Maybe one of the suitcases was filled with presents for Rachel and her parents," Liza suggested.

I smiled at her. That was such a Liza-esque thing to say. Liza refused to see the bad in anyone.

But I had a feeling with Madison, even she might have met her match.

"I doubt it," I said honestly. "I don't get the feeling Madison's the gift-giving kind."

"She's coming to our tree-trimming party on Christmas Eve," Marilyn said.

"Rachel asked if we'd invite her, so we did," Carolyn added. She flipped her long blond hair over her shoulder. She was wearing little red-and-green Santa Claus post earrings. They actually would have matched her new necklace really nicely, but she wasn't wearing it today.

"It was nice of you guys to include Madison," I told them.

"If we didn't, Rachel said she couldn't come," Carolyn explained.

"And this way we can all be together at the party," Marilyn finished her sister's thought.

I wish Marc felt that was important, I thought to myself. But out loud all I said was, "Madison will be well behaved at your party. She'll have to be. We outnumber her."

"Where is she, anyway?" Felicia asked. She scanned the ice for a minute, looking for Madison's sky blue ski jacket with the soft furry collar. When she finally spotted her, Felicia's face took on a decidedly angry look. "What's she doing with Josh?" she demanded.

We all looked across the ice. Sure enough, there was Madison, getting up from a spill on the ice. She was holding on to Josh's arm, and obviously convincing him to help her learn to skate.

"Oh, that's not happening," Felicia said. "I'm going over there!"

"Uh-oh," Liza said.

"I haven't seen her that mad in a long time," I pointed out.

"Everyone here knows Josh is her boyfriend," Marilyn said.

"But Madison doesn't," Carolyn reminded her sister.

"Maybe we ought to skate over there," Liza said. "Just to make sure things are okay."

"Good idea," I agreed. I turned to the twins. "Are you guys coming?"

Marilyn shook her head. "I'm going to go get some hot chocolate," she said. "I'm kind of cold."

"Where's your warm hat?" I asked her. I was actually surprised to see her not wearing it.

"I forgot it," she told me.

"I told you you should have gone back inside to get it," Carolyn reminded her sister.

"I'm okay," Marilyn said. "I just want hot chocolate."

"I could go for one, too," Carolyn agreed.

"See you guys later," they both said as they skated off toward the exit.

As the twins left the ice, Liza and I hurried over to where Felicia, Josh, and Madison were standing. Felicia was standing next to Josh. She had a smile on her face. To someone who didn't know her that well, Felicia looked very friendly. But I've known Felicia since kindergarten. I can tell when she's faking it.

"Josh is such a good skater, I thought maybe he could teach me a few things," Madison was telling Felicia as Liza and I arrived on the scene.

"I think you'd be better off with a real teacher," Felicia replied in as sweet of a voice as she could muster. "They're all around the ice. You can pick out the instructors because they're in green vests."

"Oh," Madison said. "I just figured it would be more fun to have someone my own age teach me to skate."

"Did you ask Rachel?" Felicia wondered. "She is your cousin, after all."

I looked over at Josh. He was obviously feeling

really uncomfortable. All he'd done was help some-one up from a fall on the ice. And now all this was happening. Something inside me made me feel I just had to rescue him from the mess he was in.

"I'll help you," I told Madison.

Madison gave me an odd look. It was pretty clear I wasn't exactly the skating partner she'd had in mind. But there was no way she could get out of it. So she shrugged her shoulders and said, "Okay, I guess. If you think you're good enough to help me."

That made me really mad. Considering how wet the seat of her pants was, it was clear anyone on the ice today was a better skater than she was. I was certainly qualified to teach her the basics.

"It's not that hard," I assured her. "You just move one foot in front of the other. It's kind of like walking, but with a glide between steps."

My friends all skated off as Madison and I gin-gerly made our way around the perimeter of the rink, stopping every few seconds for her to grab on to the rail and complain about something.

"The ice is very crowded," she moaned as we slowly skated toward one of the walls. "And there are a lot of little kids around."

"Skating's a big deal around here," I explained. "We all learn to skate when we're little. I guess where you live people learn to surf when they're little."

Madison nodded. "I've surfed a few times," she said. "It's really fun. And it's definitely a warmer sport."

"You'll warm up when you start to skate a little faster," I said. "Look at those kids in the center of the ice. They're not even wearing coats, but they're really moving."

"Those are nice dresses," Madison remarked, checking out the skating skirts some of the girls were wearing. "How come you and Rachel aren't dressed up in those?"

"I don't know," I told her. "Skating dresses aren't really my thing. I'm not here for the fashion. I'm just here to have a good time."

"Look at the pink-and-white dress that girl is wearing," Madison said, pointing to the far corner of the ice. "It's gorgeous."

I looked over at the girl Madison had been pointing to and frowned. As if it wasn't bad enough that I was stuck here on the ice with Rachel's conceited California cousin, now I knew that Addie

Wilson was at the skating rink. And not just Addie, either. Dana, Sabrina, and Maya were with her as well.

The Pops weren't skating, though. They were just standing around, letting other people admire their skating skirts. And people were definitely admiring them. Madison was just one of many who were staring at the Pops with a look of admiration in their eyes.

"Do those kids go to your school?" Madison asked me.

I nodded. "Yeah."

Suddenly Madison seemed interested in my life. "Are you friends with them?" she asked me excitedly.

"No," I told her. "They're . . ." I paused for a minute, trying to figure out a good way to describe the Pops. "They're a tight group. They just hang out with each other."

"Oh." Madison definitely sounded disappointed.

Amazing. The Pops had managed to work their magic from all the way across the ice. Madison had joined the ranks of the hundreds of kids who wished they could be one of the Joyce Kilmer Middle School Pops. Madison was definitely snobby and spoiled enough to be a Pop. Her only problem was that she was Rachel's cousin. And since Rachel wasn't a Pop, Madison didn't have a shot at breaking into their very exclusive group.

"I'm getting hungry," Madison said, going back into complaint mode. "Do they have decent food here?"

"Sure," I told her. "There's a snack bar with hamburgers, hot dogs, grilled cheese, pretzels, soda, and hot chocolate."

"I think a hamburger would hit the spot right now," Madison said.

So Madison and I got off the ice and made our way over to the snack bar. "I'll have a hot dog and an order of cheese fries," I told the woman behind the counter. All that skating had made me kind of hungry, too.

"And I'll have a hamburger," Madison said. "Medium rare. With just a touch of pink in the middle."

The woman behind the counter started to laugh. "Medium rare?" she asked Madison. "Are you kidding me?"

Madison shook her head. "Why would I be kidding you?"

The woman moved to the side so Madison could get a good look at the rows of burgers on the snack bar grill. "We cook 'em all the same way, honey."

"Oh," Madison said. She didn't sound the least bit embarrassed.

"Order it anyway," I told her. "The burgers here are awesome. Trust me."

"Okay," Madison said, but she sounded doubtful. "I'll have a hamburger and an orange soda."

"Coming right up," the woman behind the counter told us. "That'll be six dollars each."

Madison and I paid the woman and then waited for our food. When it was ready we took our trays and looked for a place to sit. I noticed Liza, Marilyn, Carolyn, and Marc sitting at a table near the back of the room. I didn't particularly want to sit near Marc, but I also didn't want to have to spend my snack time hanging out with Madison by myself. Chloe and Rachel were still skating with Felicia and Josh. So I chose the lesser of the two evils, and led Madison to the back of the snack bar where my friends were all sitting.

"Ooh, cheese fries," Marilyn squealed as I sat down.

"Can I have one?" Carolyn asked.

"Help yourselves," I told them. "They gave me a huge portion."

"They make great fries at this rink," Liza said. "And the pretzels are good, too. They're not too salty."

Marc took a sip of his milk shake and then turned to Madison. "You must be Rachel's cousin. I'm Marc. It's nice to meet you."

I sighed slightly. I didn't think meeting Madison was particularly nice. Then again, I didn't think Marc was too nice of a guy lately. They were perfect for each other.

"You're the one having a party on New Year's Eve," Madison said.

Marc nodded. "Yup. You and Rachel are coming, right?"

"I guess so," Madison told him. "It's not like there's going to be a whole lot of other things to do around here on New Year's Eve."

Now I was *really* mad. Marc had invited Madison – who he didn't even know – to his party, but he'd left *me* out. And Madison was going to go to the party even though she obviously didn't want to go at all. This was unbelievable. It was almost like I had suddenly moved into some alternate reality, where a stranger like Madison was suddenly doing everything I wanted to do.

"There's plenty to do around here," I told Madison. "Marc's party is just one of a million options."

Marc looked at me really strangely, and then he looked hurt. I couldn't believe him. He was acting like *I* had hurt *his* feelings, instead of the other way around. Yeah, like he was the one being excluded around here. *Right.*

As if things weren't bad enough, my mother suddenly appeared at the table with her car keys in hand. Now, it's not like I don't like my mom, or that my friends don't like her. It was just weird having her suddenly appear out of nowhere. She was at least thirty minutes earlier than she had said she'd be when she agreed to pick me up.

"Hi, Jen," my mom greeted me. "Hi, everybody."

"Hello, Mrs. McAfee," my friends replied.

"Listen, Jen, sorry I'm early, but I've got to take you home now," my mom told me. "I have about a million errands to run before Christmas Eve." She smiled mysteriously. "And a few of them involve your gifts, so I know you want me to get to the stores as soon as possible."

I laughed. My mother sure knew how to get to

me. "Okay, just let me throw away my trash and turn in my skates and we can leave," I told her.

"Great," my mom said. "And while you're at it, find Addie and tell her it's time to go. I promised her mom I'd give her a ride home, too."

Addie? As if this skating trip hadn't turned out badly enough, now I had to sit next to Addie in the back of my car and pretend to be nice to her.

My friends clearly understood my predicament. They all shot me sympathetic glances from across the table. Of course, none of them said anything about it. They knew better than to make any cracks or criticisms of Addie in front of an adult.

And so did I. I had no choice. I had to go find Addie, tell her it was time to leave, and endure a few disses from the other Pops while I was doing it. *Grrrr.* This was not the way I'd hoped my vacation would start. But then again, there was a positive side to all of this. I figured things had nowhere to go from here but up.

Chapter
SIX

AND I WAS RIGHT. Things did get better as soon as I got home. I turned on my computer, and there was an invitation for a video chat with Sam.

"Hi!" I shouted as soon as Sam's image popped onto the screen. She'd only been gone a day, but I was so excited to see her, it was as if she'd been gone for a whole month.

"Hi!" Sam exclaimed back. (Apparently, she felt the same way.) "How's your holiday so far?"

For a minute, I thought about telling her all the awful things that had happened, like not getting invited to Marc's party, and how horrible Rachel's cousin was, and how I had to endure an entire car ride home from the rink with Addie Wilson. But I figured there was no reason for me to moan and groan and act all grumpy when Sam looked so happy.

"It's been pretty good," I told her. "I just got back from the skating rink. It was packed with people. What are you up to?"

"Mum and Dad and I are going to a late supper at my aunt's," Sam said. "But I wish I could stay home. I'm positively knackered."

"Positively what?" I asked her.

"Knackered," Sam said. "You know, exhausted. It was a long flight last night, and I spent a lot of today shopping on Carnaby Street with some of my mates."

Mates. I knew that one. It meant *friends.* "I bet they were happy to see you."

"They were," Sam said. "And I was happy to see them. I have to tell you, Jenny, that when I first found out I wouldn't be spending my holiday with you lot, I was positively gutted. But now I'm kind of glad we came over here for a while."

I wasn't surprised that Sam was happy to be in London over vacation. I could understand that. But I was amazed at how different she sounded already. She'd only been back in England one day, but already her accent had gotten thicker, and she was back to using some of the British slang she'd used when she'd first moved to the U.S. It was as if in just one day, all of the American stuff she'd picked up had completely disappeared.

"Listen, Jenny, I have to run," Sam told me.

"We're leaving in ten minutes, and I have to dig my black jumper out of the bottom of my suitcase."

A jumper was a sweater. I'd learned that after months of mall shopping with Sam and her mom . . . I mean her *mum*. "Are you wearing it with your red skinny jeans?" I asked her.

Sam nodded. "Yep. And my new black trainers. My aunt keeps things casual at her house."

"Your new black what?"

"Trainers," Sam repeated. "Sneakers."

"Oh," I said. "That sounds cute. Have fun tonight."

"You, too," Sam said. "And keep me posted on everything going on there."

"You got it," I assured her.

I felt so much better after talking to Sam. Sure, it would have been great if she'd been right there in my room, but it was still fun to be able to chat face-to-face on the computer. It was kind of like she was still here. Well, sort of, anyway.

As soon as Sam signed off, I switched my attention to my next holiday activity. I wanted to make an ornament to bring to the tree-trimming party Marilyn and Carolyn were throwing. Of course, I had no idea how to make a tree ornament. Luckily, I knew where to find out: middleschoolsurvival.com.

Sure enough, my favorite website had plenty of suggestions and directions for making Christmas tree decorations. I glanced at a few of them, looking for an ornament that was perfect, but not too difficult to make. Eventually, I found one that I knew the twins would love.

A Sweet and Spicy Christmas Ornament!

Spice up your tree with this sweet-smelling orange-clove ornament.

YOU WILL NEED:

1 orange, 1 jar of cloves, approximately 3 feet of festive, 1-inch-wide ribbon, and a hot glue gun

HERE'S WHAT YOU DO:

1. Choose a nicely shaped, thin-skinned orange.
2. Ask an adult to help you hot glue a one-inch-wide ribbon around the orange. You will use this ribbon to hang the ornament from your tree. To make sure the ribbon stays

secure, crisscross the ribbon into an X shape
and tie a bow at the top.

3. Poke the cloves into the orange. Poke them
   deep, so that only the large top of the clove
   can be seen. How many cloves you use is up
   to you. You can cover the orange completely
   in cloves, or use the cloves to make patterns.

4. Use the bow part of your ribbon to hang the
   orange–clove ornament from your tree.

I spent the rest of the evening gathering up the
materials from around the house and the kitchen,
and making an orange-clove ornament. By the time
I was finished I was sure I had created the perfect
gift. It smelled so wonderful – a little spicy and a
little sweet.

But I also decided that I wasn't going to give
this orange-clove ornament to the twins, because
Christmas Eve wasn't until Monday night, and it
was only Saturday. I had a whole day in between.
By then the orange might be a little dried out. So
I hung this ornament on my tree, and made plans
to create an identical one for the twins on Monday

morning. That way their gift would smell as sweet and fresh as possible.

Okay, so on Monday I was making an ornament and going to a party. But I still wasn't sure what I was going to do on Sunday yet. But that's the good thing about vacation. You have lots of free time, so you don't have to plan things way in advance. You can just play it by ear.

Actually, it was Rachel who came up with a plan for Sunday. She invited Chloe and me to go to the movies with her and Madison. The truth is, I didn't really feel like being around Madison again. But after Chloe called me, I felt like I sort of had to go.

"I said yes before I realized Madison would be coming, too," Chloe told me on the phone.

"Madison is her guest for the whole vacation, Chloe," I reminded her. "Of course she'd be coming."

"I guess I just sort of pushed Madison out of my mind," Chloe explained. "I was half asleep when Rachel called me."

I didn't blame Chloe for forgetting about Madison. She was the kind of person anyone would want to forget about if she could.

"I was awake when she called," I told Chloe. "But I couldn't come up with a good excuse for not going with her. And besides, I feel really badly for Rachel. She's stuck with Madison."

"I know," Chloe agreed. "The least we can do is go with her so she has some normal people to talk to before the movie starts."

"Normal?" I teased. "When's the last time anyone called you normal, Chloe?"

Chloe giggled. "You've got me there."

"Rachel's mom is picking me up in fifteen minutes," I reminded her. "I still have to get dressed. So I'd better hang up."

"Okay," Chloe agreed. "I'll see you in a few minutes. And if we're lucky, Madison has decided to be nice today."

"Maybe," I said, trying to sound hopeful, even though I wasn't.

I knew Madison hadn't changed the minute we stepped into the movie theater. She took one look at the candy counter and rolled her eyes. "I can't believe they don't sell gummy bears here. I always have gummy bears at the movie theater near my house."

"They have gummy *worms*," Rachel's mother pointed out. "Isn't that the same thing?"

"Not at all," Madison said with a sigh. "I guess I'll just have a popcorn. I hope it's fresh, though. I hate when they let the popcorn just sit around all day getting stale."

"It looks like it's popping right now," I said, pointing to the giant popcorn machine behind the counter.

"I think that's just for show," Madison replied. "I wonder if they have real butter. That's what they have at my regular movie theater. Of course, I don't know what you people are used to."

I could see the furor rising in Chloe. Her cheeks were flushed and her eyes sparkled angrily. The way Madison had said "you people" was incredibly condescending. But even Chloe – who was afraid of no one – wasn't about to be rude to Madison in front of Rachel's mother.

Still, Rachel's mother was a little tired of Madison, too. I could tell by the way her shoulders sort of sagged, and how she took a short quick breath before reaching into her wallet and pulling out some cash. "Here, Rachel, you pay for everyone," she said. "I'm going to go find a seat in the back. You girls can sit wherever you like."

As Rachel's mother walked away, Madison shook her head in disapproval. "I don't know why Aunt Grace has to be here, anyway. It's not like we're babies or anything. My mom doesn't come to the movies with me when I go with my friends.

Just like the Pops, I thought ruefully to myself. I knew all too well that Dana, Addie, Sabrina, Maya, and Claire never went to the movies with an adult. Once again I found myself thinking just how much Madison had in common with that group of snobs.

"You guys want to sit all the way up front?" Chloe asked us. "That's always fun."

Madison shook her head. "I hate sitting up front. My neck always hurts by the end of the movie."

"I would think your neck would hurt anywhere you sat," Chloe said. "I mean, it takes a lot of effort to spend your whole life looking down your nose at everyone."

Madison's eyes opened wide. "Are you saying I'm a snob?"

"What do you think?" Chloe asked her.

Madison rolled her eyes. "I think an argument with you isn't worth my time," she said. She walked up to the counter and smiled sweetly at the guy selling the snacks. "I'll have a small popcorn with butter," she said.

Chloe wasn't about to let Madison end the conversation that way. She opened her mouth to say something, but Rachel pulled her a few inches away from Madison so her cousin couldn't hear a word she was saying.

"Please, Chloe," Rachel whispered. "Just let it go. I can't listen to her another minute. And if you say something, then she'll say something, and it'll go on forever and ever."

Chloe looked at Rachel. I knew she could see how frustrated Rachel was with her cousin. "Okay," she said. "But I'm only keeping quiet for you. And only this once. If she starts up again . . ."

"Thanks," Rachel said sincerely. Then she added in a whisper, "You guys are the best friends in the world for coming with us today. I didn't want to be alone with her."

I nodded understandingly. I didn't blame Rachel for that. Not one bit.

That night, Chloe and I had a sleepover at my house. It was so much fun. My dad has this DVD collection of really funny Christmas Claymation cartoons from when he was a kid, and we watched them all night long. It might seem kind of weird for two sixth graders to stay up watching cartoons, but I wasn't embarrassed, at least not in front of Chloe. She never judges me. And besides, she was watching them with me. So I knew my cartoon-watching secret was safe.

Actually, Chloe had surprised me by how well she could keep a secret. She hadn't said one word to Marc about how angry I was that he hadn't invited me to his party. She hadn't even brought it up once since school let out on Friday. And I was really grateful for that.

Of course, Chloe is not known for holding things in forever. And somewhere around the middle of *Rudolph the Red-Nosed Reindeer* she said, "Are you planning on ignoring Marc at the tree-trimming party tomorrow?"

I sighed heavily. "I really don't want to talk about it, Chlo."

But Chloe wasn't about to let the conversation end there. "You can't just stop talking to him," she told me.

"Why not?" I asked her. "I'd rather do that than start a fight in the middle of the twins' party."

"But what about after the party?" Chloe asked me. "Are you just going to ignore him in school, too?"

"I guess so," I said. "He really hurt my feelings."

"Boy," Chloe said. "You sure can hold a grudge."

"I don't hold grudges," I told her. "In fact, I'm really good about not staying mad about things."

Chloe snickered.

"What's that supposed to mean?" I asked her.

"Nothing," Chloe said. "Except you're totally wrong. You hold plenty of grudges. And I can prove it."

"How are you going to do that?" I asked her.

"Easy," she said. "We're going to find a quiz on middleschoolsurvival.com. And you're going to take it. Unless you're afraid to."

"Oh *please*," I countered. "I'm not afraid. If it will prove to you that I don't hold grudges, I'd be glad to take a quiz."

"Good," Chloe said. "Then let's go up to your room and find one."

A moment later, Chloe and I were sitting in front of my computer scanning the quiz list on middleschoolsurvival.com. Sure enough, they had exactly what we were searching for.

Is Your Life a Grudge Match?

How hard do you hold on to your anger? Are you a forgiving-and-forgetting friend, or a grudge-grabbing gal? To find out how much you allow the little annoyances and arguments in your life to affect you, take some time to take this quiz.

1. You're at the movie theater when someone bumps into you, spills your popcorn all over the place, and then just walks away. How do you react?

A. Ignore them.
B. Say, "Excuse you."
C. Bump him right back.

"Well, I definitely wouldn't bump the guy right back," I told Chloe. "Because it might start a huge fight. But I don't think I'd completely ignore it, either. It's pretty rude to just pretend you didn't spill someone's popcorn all over the place. So I guess my answer is B."

"B it is," Chloe replied, clicking the mouse over the letter. The next question popped up immediately on the screen.

2. A friend borrows your sweater and forgets to give it back to you. How do you handle the situation?

A. Just replace the sweater. The other one looked better on your friend, anyway.

B. Bug her until she finally gives it back to you.

C. Go to her house, grab the sweater, and vow to never — ever — loan her anything again.

"Wow," I said, looking over the choices. "This is tough. Because I don't think I would just barge into someone's room and take something, even if it was mine. But I really hate nagging people, too. I wish there was a choice where you could go to someone's house and ask nicely for the sweater."

Chloe shook her head. "You've only got three choices."

I nodded slowly. "Well, then, I guess it has to be C, because that's closer to what I would actually do," I admitted.

Chloe clicked the mouse over the letter C, and then read the next question out loud to me.

3. Someone is spreading a rumor about your worst enemy. How do you feel about that?

A. You feel a little bad about it. No one deserves to be treated that way.

B. You don't care one way or another.

C. You're happy to hear it, and even spread the rumor to a few of your friends.

As I listened to Chloe reading the question, I remembered one time when people were spreading rumors about Addie Wilson liking a boy in the eighth grade, which I knew weren't true. When it comes to worst enemies, Addie tops my list. After the way she dropped me, who could blame me? So I didn't feel particularly badly when I heard she was in a little bit of an embarrassing situation. But I didn't spread the rumor myself. That would have been too mean.

"B," I told Chloe. "This one I'm sure of."

"Okay," she said. "B it is. Here's the next question."

4. Your math teacher wrongly accuses you of cheating in front of the whole class. But when the real cheater confesses, your teacher stops you in the hall to apologize. What's your reaction?

A. You forgive your teacher immediately. After all, everyone makes mistakes, right?

B. You thank her and say you forgive her, but you remain upset that while the accusation was public, the apology was private.

C. You make your parents go to the principal and make a formal complaint against the teacher.

"I don't think I'd want my parents charging up to school to talk to Ms. Gold for any reason," I told Chloe. "But how do you just forgive a teacher for doing something like that? That's pretty awful. My answer is B."

"Makes sense to me," Chloe agreed as she clicked the mouse and waited for the next question.

5. It's your birthday party, and all the attention is totally focused on you – until one of your guests gets into some major drama and runs to the bathroom to cry. What's your reaction?

A. You're the first one to go and help her. You feel really badly because you know how it feels to be sad at a party.

B. Do your best to ignore her and enjoy your party.

C. Tell her to go home and do her crying in private.

I smiled. This one was easy for me. I'm not big on being the center of attention. But I am *huge* on helping my friends when they're having a crisis. In fact, I'm usually the one they turn to. (Well, I'm the one they turn to when Liza's not around, anyway. She's the most levelheaded advice giver in our group of friends.) "A," I told Chloe proudly.

"I knew you were going to say that," Chloe replied with a laugh. She clicked her mouse and we waited for a minute as a new frame popped up on the screen.

You answered: B, C, B, B, A

What do your answers say about you?

Mostly A's: Wow, talk about being a forgiving friend! You're clearly a very generous and kind person who has learned the art of moving on.

Mostly B's: This is where most people fall on the grudge-holding scale. You try to forgive, but sometimes you find that letting things go is harder than you'd like to think. However, now that you know this about yourself, maybe it will be easier for you to be a little more understanding and forgiving in the future.

Mostly C's: Wow! Those heavy grudges you're holding must really be weighing you down. Apparently you find it hard to forgive people once they've crossed you. But remember: Someday, you may be on the other side of that equation, and you'll want to be forgiven. Try to give others that same courtesy.

"Well, I didn't do too badly," I told Chloe. "I forgive some of the time."

"That's true," Chloe agreed. "But you also still hold some grudges."

"I know," I admitted. "I don't think I'll ever forgive Addie for what she did to me. I have actually tried to forgive her a few times, but then she always does something mean and I start hating her again."

"I don't blame you for hating Addie," Chloe assured me. "And I don't really care if you hold a grudge against her, because I don't like her, either."

I giggled. That was such a Chloe thing to say. A grudge was okay as long as it was against someone *she* also had issues with.

"But I do like Marc," Chloe continued. "He's not mean to you all the time. He just did this one little thing."

"It's not such a little thing, Chloe," I said. "I'm really hurt."

"But if you just talk to him and ask him . . ." Chloe began.

I shook my head. "I'm not going to ask him why he didn't invite me to the party," I told her for what felt like the one thousandth time. "But I won't be mean to him all night at the tree-trimming party, either. I don't want to make everyone else uncomfortable."

The truth was, I also didn't want to embarrass myself by letting everyone know I was the only person in our whole group who wasn't invited. So far no one else seemed to be aware of that fact. Or if they were, they weren't telling me about it.

Chloe sighed heavily. "I guess that's the most I can ask for," she said slowly.

I nodded. "It's the most you're going to get," I replied.

Chapter
SEVEN

THE TREE-TRIMMING PARTY at Marilyn and Carolyn's had already started by the time I arrived at their house on Christmas Eve. I could hear the music coming from inside the house as I walked up the path to the front door. And when Marilyn and Carolyn opened the door, it nearly blasted me away. *"Oh the weather outside is frightful, but the fire is so delightful . . ."*

Actually, the weather was anything *but* frightful. In fact, it was kind of warm out. It didn't seem like we were going to have a white Christmas after all. Which kind of made me sad. I feel like Christmas really should be all white and snowy, but tonight I wasn't even wearing my warmest coat. And apparently, I wasn't the only one who felt really bummed out about that.

"I'm so glad you're here," Marilyn told me as I followed her into the house. "Rachel's cousin Madison is making everyone nuts."

"She keeps complaining about how she came

here for snow on Christmas, and it's not happening," Carolyn explained.

"Like that's something we can control," Marilyn added, shaking her head. "Give me a break."

"We're all taking turns talking to her so no one has to be around her for very long," Carolyn told me.

I nodded understandingly. Madison could be a real pain when she was miserable. Which, from the few times I'd been around her, seemed to be all of the time. "I'll take my shift," I assured my friends. "I'm pretty used to her at this point."

"Thank you!" both twins said at once.

As I followed Marilyn and Carolyn into the house, I pulled my handmade ornament from my coat pocket. "This is for your Christmas tree," I told them.

"Cool," Marilyn said. "It smells amazing."

"You can hang it on any branch you like," Carolyn said.

Not that there were that many choices of places to hang my orange-clove ornament. The tree in the twins' living room was really big, but it was absolutely covered in tinsel, Christmas balls, and all sorts of angels, snowflakes, and other Christmas trimmings. I guessed that all of the ornaments were the result of years and years of parties. Finally I found a spot for my orange-clove ornament near the center of the tree, right next to an ornament of a cat wearing a Santa Claus cap.

"That smells so nice," Liza said as she walked over to greet me.

"Thanks," I said with a proud smile. Already the smell of the oranges and cloves were mixing with the pine scent of the tree to create a very Christmassy scent.

"Do you believe how many people are here?" Liza asked me, looking around.

The party was definitely a big one. My whole group of friends had already arrived, and there were also a lot of adults milling around. I also saw a couple of younger kids running up and down the stairs of the house. I figured they were probably family friends or relatives.

"I heard Madison's really being a pain tonight," I said to Liza.

Liza didn't reply at first. I could tell she was trying to find a nicer way to put it. That was Liza, always looking for the good in people. But sometimes that goodness was pretty hard to find.

"She's a little better now," Liza said finally. "She's been on her cell phone for a while. I think some of her friends from California are calling to wish her a Merry Christmas."

"Speaking of which," I said with a laugh, "Merry Christmas, Liza."

"Merry Christmas to you, too," Liza said.

Just then Rachel came hurrying over, with Josh and Felicia trailing behind her. "Jenny, you're here!" Rachel said excitedly. "I'm so glad you made it. We've been here forever and I've been looking all over for you. Did you taste the cupcakes yet? They're incredible! Oooh, look. Candy canes! I'll be right back." And with that, she took off toward the back of the room, where a bouquet of candy canes was sitting on a table.

I looked over at Felicia and Josh. "What's with her?" I asked them.

"Way too much sugar," Felicia told me. "She's literally bouncing off the walls."

"It's like someone let her out of a cage or something," I joked.

"You're not kidding," Josh told me. "Apparently, Rachel's mom spent all day today getting Christmas dinner ready for tomorrow, so she was too busy to drive anywhere. That meant Rachel and Madison were stuck inside, *together*, with nothing to do."

"Oh, boy," I groaned, imagining just what that must have been like.

"I bet Madison's a Pop back in California," Josh said. "She acts just like one."

"I bet she's a Pop *wannabe*," Felicia corrected him.

I thought about saying, "Who isn't?" But I stopped myself. I didn't want to admit to my friends that from time to time I wondered what it would feel like to be a Pop. I figured pretty much everyone had felt that way once or twice. So I couldn't blame Madison if she really was just a Pop wannabe back home.

Still, it didn't mean we had to enjoy her company. "Being around Madison is even worse than having to spend time with the Pops," I told Felicia and Josh. "Rachel can't walk away from her or say anything mean back to her. She sort of has to just sit there and take whatever Madison dishes out because she's her cousin."

"Rachel must be really relieved to have all of us around now," Liza pointed out.

Before I could answer, Marc walked over to where Liza, Felicia, Josh, and I were standing. "Hey, you guys, what's happening?"

I stood there for a minute, working hard to force

a smile to my lips. After all, I'd promised Chloe that I would try not to hold a grudge against Marc. But that wasn't easy. Just the sight of him made me feel all angry and confused. Still, I managed to say, "Not much. Just enjoying the holiday party."

"Yeah, parties are awesome," Marc agreed. He smiled at Liza, Felicia, and Josh. "I can't wait for mine. It's not going to be as big as this one, but . . ."

That did it! I'd tried to be forgiving. I'd tried not to hold a grudge. But Marc was being a real jerk! Why was he throwing his party in my face like this? That was the meanest thing anyone had ever done to me. And considering I knew people like Addie, Claire, and Dana, that was really saying something. I no longer cared what I had promised Chloe. I was mad at Marc and I was going to stay that way!

"I have to go find Madison," I told my friends (and my ex-friend, Marc). "It's my turn to hang out with her."

Before any of them could say or ask me anything — or even worse, try to stop me — I raced off to find Rachel's cousin. Amazingly enough, spending a few minutes with Madison would be better than being in the same space with Marc! Of course, that wasn't saying much.

I found Madison hiding in the kitchen. She was talking to someone on her cell phone and didn't even seem to notice I'd entered the room. "I'm telling you, Casey, this is the worst Christmas ever," she said. "I'm at this dorky party where I barely know anyone. There're all these cupcakes that aren't from Frostings." She paused for a minute as she listened to something her friend was saying on the other end. "No, I don't think they have any designer bakeries in this ridiculously boring town."

Grrr. I wanted to scream out that those cupcakes had been made at the bakery Marilyn and Carolyn's parents owned, and that they were probably the best cupcakes made anywhere – which Madison would've known had she bothered to try one. But I didn't say anything. I didn't feel like giving her the satisfaction of knowing her constant put-downs had annoyed me.

"I wish I could go home," Madison continued. "But my mom and dad are still in the islands, so I'm stuck here." She looked up finally, and spotted me nearby. "Listen, Case, I gotta go. Call me later and tell me what you got for Christmas, okay?"

"You didn't have to hang up," I told Madison.

Madison shoved her phone in her pocket. "It's

okay," she said. "We were pretty much done talking, anyway."

"You're not having a great time here, are you?" I asked her.

Madison just sort of shrugged. "Whatever," she said.

I knew what she meant. I was kind of in a "whatever" sort of mood, too, now that Marc had ruined my evening. So I just stood there next to Madison staring into space. I didn't really have a whole lot to say to her. She didn't have much to say to me, either.

So I was kind of glad when Liza came rushing into the kitchen to find me. "Come on, you guys," she said. "It's present time."

My eyes opened wide with surprise. "Presents?" I asked, shocked. "I didn't know we were supposed to bring presents."

"Relax. Marilyn and Carolyn are going to give *us* presents," Liza explained. "Just little things. They do it every year."

"Oh. I didn't know," I said. I turned to Madison. "I just met the twins this year, and this is my first tree-trimming party here, too."

"So go get your gift," Madison said. "I'll be fine here."

"You have to come, too," Liza said. "I'm sure they have something for you."

"You think?" Madison asked doubtfully.

"I *know*," Liza assured her. "Marilyn and Carolyn never leave anyone out. They're not like that."

"Unlike Marc," I mumbled under my breath.

"What?" Madison asked me.

"Oh, nothing," I said quickly. A red flush rose up in my cheeks. I hadn't realized I had been speaking out loud.

I was glad that Liza was already heading into the next room. That meant she hadn't heard me. I forced a smile and followed behind her. Madison came with me. She actually seemed almost excited to see what the twins had gotten her.

"This is so cute!" I heard Chloe exclaim as she pulled a small ornament from a box. "It's a dog bone."

"We thought you could hang it on your tree as Bingo's ornament," Marilyn told her.

"It's for his very first Christmas at your house," Carolyn added.

"He's going to love it," Chloe said. "Thank you so much."

"Oh, look, I got a dreidel," Josh said as he unwrapped a large, hollow, green plastic top with Hebrew letters. "And it's got chocolate in it," he added as he removed the top of the dreidel and peeked inside.

"It's still Hanukkah, isn't it?" Marilyn asked him.

"We thought it was," Carolyn added.

"Yes," Josh assured them. "There are still two more days. Thanks so much."

"Great!" the twins exclaimed happily.

I watched as Felicia and Rachel both unwrapped basketball ornaments, which were perfect for them, since they were the only two sixth graders on our school's varsity basketball team. Liza's ornament was shaped like an artist's pallet, and Marc's was shaped like a camera because he wanted to be a movie director when he grew up. (Not that I cared anymore about what Marc got or did.) I could tell the twins had spent a lot of time thinking about what gifts to get each of us, so I was pretty excited when Carolyn handed me a box wrapped in green-and-red shimmery paper. I didn't even try to be neat about unwrapping the gift. I just tore the paper off and ripped the box open.

"Oh, it's so cute!" I exclaimed excitedly. Then I held up my ornament for everyone else to see. It was a grandfather clock with a little white mouse on it.

"It's the mouse running up the clock," Carolyn said.

"From 'Hickory Dickory Dock,'" Marilyn added.

"It's perfect!" I exclaimed. "Thanks so much. I can't wait to show it to Cody and Sam."

"Who are Cody and Sam?" Madison asked.

"Her pet mice," Rachel explained.

Madison made a face. "You have mice?" she asked me.

I nodded. "Two of them. The live in a cage in my room."

Madison looked slightly grossed out at that. Not that I was surprised. Most people have that reaction when they hear I have pet mice. At least until they meet Cody and Sam. Once people see how cute and soft they are, they can't help but love them.

"Open your gift, Maddie," Rachel urged. Then, noticing her cousin's expression, she corrected herself. "I mean, *Madison*."

"Okay," Madison said. She unwrapped her gift and pulled a surfboard-shaped ornament from the box.

"We figured since you're from Los Angeles you must surf," Carolyn told her.

"Or at least you must know someone who surfs," Marilyn said.

"Yeah, I know some surfers," Madison said. She didn't sound very happy. She didn't say thank you, either.

"Don't you like your gift?" Marilyn asked her.

"It's nice," Madison said. "But I don't have a tree to hang it on."

"Can't you hang it on Rachel's tree?" Carolyn wondered.

"Sure. But then it's a gift for *her* family, isn't it?" Madison asked.

Marilyn and Carolyn didn't say anything. Not that I blamed them. What can you say to that?

"Didn't you guys get each other anything?" Liza asked the twins, clearly trying to change the subject.

Marilyn and Carolyn cheered instantly. "You're going to love what I got you!" they both shouted out at exactly the same time. Then they both broke out into giggles and ran to find their gifts under the tree.

"Do they do that all the time?" Madison asked her cousin.

Rachel nodded. "It's a twin thing."

"It's a *weird* thing," Madison countered.

"I think it's cool," I told Madison.

Before Madison could say anything else, Marilyn and Carolyn reappeared, boxes in hand. We all watched as they handed each other their presents.

Carolyn opened her gift first. She opened the box and pulled out a piece of red-and-green beaded jewelry. "It's a bracelet," Carolyn said.

"Uh-huh," Marilyn told her excitedly. "It matches your new necklace."

"Oh, yeah, it does match it," Carolyn said. Surprisingly, she didn't sound very excited. "Open your gift," she told her sister.

Marilyn opened the lid of her long gift box. "It's a wool scarf," Marilyn said, sounding even less excited about her gift than Carolyn had.

"It goes with your new hat," Carolyn told her. "I went to the same store. You're going to look so cool in a matching hat and scarf."

Marilyn took a deep breath. "Well, the thing is . . ." she said slowly. "I don't have the hat any-more. I kind of sold it."

"You *what*?" Carolyn asked her.

"I sold it to Gina Carpenter. You know, that eighth grader with the dark hair," Marilyn said. "That's why I wasn't wearing it at the skating rink the other day. I didn't have it anymore. I needed the money to get you the bracelet to match your necklace."

"Oh, no," Carolyn groaned.

"It's okay," Marilyn told her sister. "I can wear the scarf by itself."

"It's not that," Carolyn replied.

"Then what's wrong?" Marilyn asked.

"I returned my necklace to get the money to buy you the scarf," Carolyn told her. "That's why I'm wearing my reindeer pin tonight."

That's when Chloe burst out laughing. "Wait, let me get this straight," she said. "Marilyn, you sold your hat to get the money to buy Carolyn a bracelet that matches the necklace that she doesn't have anymore, because she returned it so she could buy you the scarf to match your hat."

The twins looked at each other. "That's pretty much it," they said together.

"Wow," Chloe said. "For two people who are usually so totally in tune with each other, you really blew it this time."

"I guess our twin radar was off," Carolyn said.

"*Majorly* off," Marilyn agreed. "But I really do love this scarf. I don't need a matching hat to wear with it."

"Same with the bracelet," Carolyn agreed. "I can wear my pretty gold chain necklace with it. Or maybe some red earrings."

"I'm going to wear my new scarf when we go caroling," Marilyn said.

"Merry Christmas!" the twins said as they hugged each other. They looked so incredibly happy. And their happiness was infectious. It was absolutely impossible for anyone to be unhappy or cranky around them.

Just then Madison's cell phone rang. She pulled it from her pocket and checked the caller ID. Then, without even excusing herself, she walked away from my group of friends.

"Hi, Jasmine," I heard her say. "Yeah. I'm still here. And in a few minutes I'm going to be stuck going out caroling with my cousin. Can you believe that?"

I sighed. Okay, I guess it was absolutely impossible for *almost* anyone to be unhappy or cranky. Madison was the exception . . . as usual.

Chapter
EIGHT

WE MAY NOT have had a white Christmas, but we did have a white *day after* Christmas. When I woke up on the morning of December 26 and peered out of the window beside my bed, I could see that a few inches of snow had already fallen on my front lawn. And the snow was still coming down.

Apparently, Chloe saw snow on her lawn, too, because she called me before I was even out of bed. "Good morning," she greeted me as I answered the call. Her voice was full of excitement.

"Good morning, Chlo," I replied in a voice that gave away the fact that I'd only just woken up. I couldn't disguise it. Those first words you say in the morning always give you away.

"I can't believe you're still sleeping! Did you *see* what's going on out there?" Chloe asked me. "It's awesome. You've got to meet me at Fender's Hill. Everyone's going to be there."

"Everyone?" I asked her.

"Oh, yeah," Chloe told me. "Liza called me, and I called you, and you're supposed to call Rachel, who should call Felicia, and . . ."

I laughed. "I get it. We've got a phone chain going."

"So you'll call Rachel?" Chloe asked me.

"Well, I have to ask my mom first," I told Chloe. "She gets a little freaked out about how steep Fender's Hill is. But I think she'll say it's okay."

A few minutes later, I was still hoping my mom would be alright with my going sledding with my friends on Fender's Hill. I'd asked her permission to do that during the last snowstorm we had, and I'd almost gotten her to say yes, but I'd had a little complication — Addie Wilson. I'd been stuck with her all day because her mother had to work and we didn't have school. I don't know why parents can't figure out that just because they're friends, that doesn't mean their kids are, too, but Mrs. Wilson had dropped Addie at our house. And that whole day, Addie had made it a point to make my life miserable — including putting the kibosh on any sledding. And since she didn't want to go, my mother had said I couldn't go, either.

But I didn't have Addie around to ruin anything

today. And so I was very hopeful as I raced down the stairs to ask permission.

My mom and dad were sitting at the kitchen table having coffee and reading the paper when I arrived.

"Good morning, sleepyhead," my dad greeted me with a smile. "You sure slept in. It's almost nine."

"Sleeping late's one of the best parts of being on vacation," I told him. "The other best part is hanging around with my friends. Which reminds me . . ."

"Uh-oh," my mother joked. "Here it comes. Jenny's got her I-want-to-ask-you-something-you-might-not-like face on."

"Oh, it's no big deal," I assured her. "I just want to know if it's okay to go sledding with my friends . . . on Fender's Hill." I added the last part almost like it was an afterthought.

But my mother didn't see it as an afterthought. "Jenny, you know I hate Fender's Hill. It's very steep and bumpy and . . ."

"But, Mom, you don't get all freaked out when we go skiing," I insisted. "Fender's Hill isn't even as steep as a bunny slope! And all of my friends will be there. *With* our cell phones, so we can call if there's a problem. And besides, I'm in sixth grade now – *middle school.* I'm practically almost an adult."

That last part made my parents laugh. It kind of made me laugh, too. I knew I'd gone a little too far. But I was making a point.

And apparently my mom had gotten it. "I didn't say you couldn't go," she said slowly. "I just said it worried me." She looked over at my dad. "What do you think?"

My dad shot me a grin. "I think Jenny will be okay," he said.

My mother sighed heavily. "Okay, you can go. Just call me every now and then, okay?"

"I will," I promised. I turned and started back toward the stairs.

"Hey, where are you going?" my mother asked.

"To get dressed and call Rachel," I answered.

"Oh no you don't," my mom insisted. "Even 'almost adults' need to eat breakfast before they head out to go sledding. Sit down and I'll make you some oatmeal."

About an hour later, with a stomach full of oatmeal, and wearing the brand-new snow pants I'd received for Christmas, I met up with my friends on Fender's Hill.

"Hey, Jenny," Chloe called out as I arrived. "We're over here."

I looked through the sea of kids who had gathered at Fender's Hill that morning and finally spotted Chloe's bright yellow down jacket. She was standing at the top of the hill with Liza, Felicia, and Josh.

"Hi, guys," I said as I dragged my bright green plastic snow disc over to where they were sledding.

"I didn't think you were ever going to get here," Chloe said.

"My mom had to make sure I had a good breakfast," I told her. My friends all laughed. They knew exactly what I meant. In some ways, all moms are the same.

"Where's everyone else?" I asked.

"The twins went skiing with their cousins," Liza said.

"Oh," I said quietly. I was a little jealous. I love skiing, and it definitely would have been fun to hit the slopes on a day like today, especially since the snow had stopped falling and the sun was struggling to peek its way out from the clouds. Still, I had to admit that being at Fender's Hill was pretty exciting, too. It was my first time at the hill, and my first time sledding without any adults around.

"I don't know where Rachel is," Felicia said. "She called me, so I figured she'd be here before me."

"Marc's on his way," Chloe said. "He had to shovel the driveway before his folks would let him come over here."

"Whatever," I said, trying hard not to roll my eyes. But Chloe caught the tone in my voice and shot me a look.

"You guys want to make a sled train?" Felicia asked, obviously oblivious to how I'd sounded at the mention of Marc's name.

"Sure!" Liza said. "Only I don't want to be the one in the front."

"That's okay," Chloe said. "I love being in the front."

We all laughed at that. Being front and center was definitely Chloe. And in this case, no one seemed to mind. We lined up our sleds, one behind the other, and got ready to slide down the big hill. But before our train could leave the station, we all heard a familiar voice shouting.

"Hey, you guys, wait for me!"

We all turned around to spot Marc running toward us, his sled in hand. He waved to us with his free hand and everyone but me waved back.

"Jump on," Liza told Marc as he reached us. "You can be the caboose."

"Okay," Marc agreed as he placed his sled behind Josh's and joined in.

I didn't have time to think about the fact that Marc had joined the train because the next minute, I was flying at top speed down Fender's Hill. When I reached the bottom, I slipped off my sled and landed face-first in a pile of snow.

I stood up and spit the snow from my mouth. Then I started laughing. "That was really fun," I told my friends.

"Let's do it again," Marc suggested.

I sighed heavily. *Way to ruin the moment, Marc*, I thought to myself. But since I knew Chloe was watching my every reaction, I replied, "I want to see how fast I can go down solo. I bet it's really amazing!"

And with that, I grabbed my green plastic sled and began trudging my way back up the hill. When I reached the top, I spotted Rachel and Madison standing there.

"I'm so glad you're here," I told Rachel.

"It took us a while," Rachel said, shooting a glance in Madison's direction. "My mom had to pick up some mint-flavored lip balm."

"I didn't want my lips to get all chapped in the cold," Madison defended herself.

"You could have used Vaseline, like I did," Rachel replied.

"That gets all gooey," Madison insisted. "Besides, we're here now, aren't we?"

"Exactly," I said, trying to break the tension between the cousins. "So come on, let's sled."

"You go first, Rachel," Madison said.

"I only have one sled," Rachel explained to me. "Madison and I have to share."

"Oh," I said. "One of you can use mine if you want to try it together."

"That's okay," Madison said. "I can wait."

"Have you ever been sledding before?" I asked her.

"I've been snow-tubing," Madison replied. "It's way cooler than this."

"I like snow-tubing, too," I told her. "But this sled goes pretty fast."

"Maybe later," Madison told me. "I have to return a phone call, anyway."

Considering the fact that Madison had been complaining that we didn't have snow on Christmas Eve, I was kind of surprised she wasn't anxious to take advantage of the snow we had now. But I wasn't questioning her. What would be the point? She'd only give me some snide answer. And besides, I was more than glad to take another trip down the hill.

"Okay, see ya in a few," I said as I sat down on my sled and whooshed my way to the base of Fender's Hill.

Eventually we did get Madison to take a few runs down the hill. She used my sled and then Rachel's sled and, eventually, even Felicia loaned hers to Madison. In the end, I was pretty sure Madison was having a good time. I swear I even saw her crack a smile once or twice. Although she went right back to her usual cranky frown the minute she caught my eye.

Still, I wasn't surprised that Madison was the first one to want to go home that afternoon. "I'm cold, I'm wet, and I'm totally bored," she told Rachel and me.

"How can you be bored when you're out sledding?" Rachel asked her.

"Because going down a hill, and then going up a

hill just to go back down again, is boring," Madison replied.

"But you said you liked snow-tubing," I pointed out. "That's the same thing."

"There's a lodge at the ski resort we go to in California," Madison told me. She looked around Fender's Hill. "There's nothing like that here. And I could go for a hot chocolate around now."

Rachel sighed. "I guess that means I'm out of here," she said reluctantly.

"I'm sorry," I told her. And I meant it.

"You want to come with us?" Rachel asked me. "You could hang out at my house for a while."

I actually wanted to stay and sled a little longer. But it seemed too cruel to make Rachel spend the whole rest of the day stuck inside with Madison. "Let me call my mom and ask her if it's okay," I said as I pulled my phone from my pocket.

A few minutes later, I was warm and dry and sitting in Rachel's living room. "You guys want to watch a movie?" Rachel asked Madison and me. "Or maybe play a game? We've got Scrabble and Monopoly."

"I love Monopoly!" I exclaimed.

"I don't," Madison told me. "It goes on and on forever, and no one ever wins."

"I win," I told her.

"Well, I'm not going to play," Madison said with such finality in her voice that I knew there was no point in arguing with her.

"How about that hot chocolate?" Rachel suggested.

"That sounds really good," I agreed.

"Do you remember how you made the hot chocolate we had the last time Felicia and I were over at your house?" Rachel asked me.

I shook my head. "Not exactly," I said. "But . . ."

"How hard can it be to make hot chocolate?" Madison interrupted us. "You just heat up some milk and pour in chocolate. If you have some marshmallows, you add them."

"Jenny's recipe for hot chocolate was better than that," Rachel told her.

"I got it off of middleschoolsurvival.com," I said. "We can find it again."

"What's middleschoolsurvival.com?" Madison asked us.

"It's this great website," I explained. "It has quizzes and recipes and craft ideas. It answers any question you could have about being in middle school."

"Oh," Madison said. She didn't sound impressed.

"Let's go find the recipe," Rachel suggested.

"You guys go ahead," Madison told us. "I'm going to go into the guest room for a few minutes. I have to call someone."

"Gee, that's new and different," Rachel murmured sarcastically under her breath as Madison wandered off.

"She does spend a lot of time on the phone," I agreed as I followed Rachel to the computer.

"She's talking to her friends in California about how much better they are than we are," Rachel said. "I am so sick of it."

"Forget her," I told my friend. "Let's find the recipe and make some hot cocoa. I guarantee Madison has never had anything better than this. Not even in Los Angeles."

Rachel smiled. "That's true," she agreed as she turned on the computer and called up our favorite website. A few seconds later, we had the recipe in hand.

Candy Cane Cocoa!

What's more wonderful on a cold winter day than hot cocoa? How about hot cocoa and candy canes? Here's how to make a sweet treat that's sure to warm you up inside! Mmmm. Delicious!
(This recipe makes four servings. Ask an adult to help you with the heating and pouring.)

HERE'S WHAT YOU NEED:

4 cups of milk, 3 1-ounce squares of semi-sweet chocolate (crushed), 4 peppermint candy canes (crushed), 1 cup whipped cream, 4 candy canes (whole).

HERE'S WHAT YOU DO:

1. Pour the milk in a saucepan and heat until hot but not boiling.
2. Use a whisk to mix in the chocolate and crushed peppermint candy until melted and smooth.

3. Pour the hot chocolate–candy cane mix into mugs and top with whipped cream.
4. Serve each mug of hot cocoa with a candy cane stirring stick.

"I'm so glad we still have plenty of candy canes around," Rachel said.

"Christmastime is definitely the season to make this hot chocolate," I agreed as I began smashing a few of the candy canes into small bits.

"Hey, Jenny," Rachel said, a smile forming across her lips. "Do you know what cannibals eat for dessert?"

"No," I replied. "What?"

"Chocolate-covered aunts!" Rachel burst out laughing at her own joke.

Personally, I thought it was kind of corny. But it was so good to hear Rachel laughing again that I joined in. Laughing's kind of contagious, anyway.

A few minutes later, Rachel's mom came into the kitchen to help us with the heating and pouring part of the recipe. She looked around and then asked us, "Where's Maddie?"

Rachel rolled her eyes. "You mean *Madison?*" she corrected her mother. "Making another phone call, of course."

Rachel's mom nodded. "She's been pretty tough this visit, I know. And you have been a very good sport."

"I know," Rachel agreed with a little laugh.

"Madison's not usually like this," Rachel's mom told me. "She's always been a happy, friendly girl."

"She has, Jenny," Rachel assured me. "When I invited you to the airport to pick her up with us, it was because I thought you'd really like her. But right now *I* don't even like her."

"Rachel!" her mom exclaimed. "That's not a nice thing to say about your own cousin."

"I just mean I don't understand how she could have changed so much," Rachel corrected herself quickly.

"She's been gone an awfully long time," I noted, trying to stop Rachel from saying anything else that might make her mom angry with her.

"Yeah," Rachel agreed. "She has."

"Her cocoa will get cold if she doesn't get out here soon," Rachel's mom said. "One of you should go get her."

"I'll go," I volunteered.

"Thanks," Rachel said. "I really appreciate it."

I didn't blame her for not volunteering to go get her cousin. Madison was sure to be annoyed at whoever went and found her. But since it was Rachel's mom who suggested it, it wasn't like we had a choice. Someone had to do it. I'd be going home soon, anyway, and then Madison would be out of my hair. So I headed off in the direction of Rachel's guest bedroom.

As I got closer, I expected to hear Madison on the phone, complaining about everyone and everything in my hometown. But that's not what I heard at all. What I heard was crying.

I stood in the hall for a minute, not sure about what to do next. If I went in there, Madison might be embarrassed. I knew I would be. And who knew what someone like Madison would do if she was caught in a situation she had wanted to keep private?

On the other hand, she sounded so incredibly upset. I couldn't just leave her there, dealing with whatever was upsetting her all alone. I'm just not that kind of person. So I peeked my head past the partially open door. "You okay?" I asked her.

Madison dabbed her eyes with a tissue and forced a crooked smile to her face. "Yeah, sure. Why wouldn't I be?" she insisted.

I had no idea why she wouldn't be happy. I also had no idea why she was crying. "You just sounded upset," I said, feebly trying to come up with an answer to her question.

"Well, you don't have to worry about it," Madison snapped at me.

Whoa. Okay then. I guess Madison didn't need — or want — my help after all. "I just came to tell you the hot chocolate was ready," I said. Then I ducked my head back out of the door and started down the hall.

Madison leaped off of the bed. "I'm sorry," she said as she approached me.

That stopped me in my tracks. It never occurred to me that Madison would ever apologize for anything she'd ever done. "It's okay," I told her.

"No, it's not," she said. "Nothing's okay."

I turned around and looked at her curiously. I had no idea what she was talking about. "Did you have a bad phone call?" I asked.

"Worse," Madison admitted. "I had no phone call. I haven't heard from my mom and dad since Christmas Eve."

Wow. "They didn't call you yesterday, on Christmas?"

Madison shook her head. "No. I guess they were too busy on the beach, or at a party or something." She paused for a minute. "Do your parents ever go on vacation without you?"

I thought for a minute. I couldn't remember any time that my parents had done that. We'd always gone away as a family. "I don't think so," I said finally. I felt kind of bad to have to say that to her, but it was the truth.

"Mine never did, either. Before now, I mean," Madison said. "And it kind of worries me."

"Worries you?" I asked. "Why?"

"Well, they've been fighting a lot lately," Madison said. "I wonder if they went away to talk about, well . . ." Her voice drifted off, and I could tell that she didn't even want to give a voice to her big fears about her parents.

"Maybe they just wanted you to have an old-fashioned Christmas in a place that gets snow," I suggested.

"That's what they *said*," Madison agreed. "But so many of my friends' parents have split up."

"That doesn't mean that your parents are

going to," I replied. "Like my grandma always says, 'Don't borrow trouble.'"

"What does that mean?" Madison asked me.

"It means don't worry about things that haven't happened yet," I said. "It's a waste of time. You can't do anything about it, anyway."

Madison nodded, taking that in. "I guess," she said slowly. Then she added, "You know, you're pretty cool."

Despite everything, I smiled at her. "Thanks."

"You won't tell my aunt or Rachel about this, will you?"

I shook my head. "I promise I won't."

"Okay," Madison said. She took a deep breath. "I can't wait to taste that hot chocolate."

"It's pretty amazing," I assured her.

"Thanks for making it," Madison told me. "And thanks for making me feel better. Sometimes it just helps to talk a little."

"I know," I agreed with a smile.

As I walked down the hallway with Madison, a thought occurred to me. Obviously Madison hadn't really been mad at Rachel, me, or any of our friends. She'd been stressed out, worried, and feeling badly about things. So she'd taken it out on us. That wasn't the nicest thing she could have done, but it happens to everyone once in a while.

And that got me wondering. Up until now, Madison had been acting so much like the Pops at our school behaved. Was it possible the Pops were mean because *they* were worried, stressed, or feeling bad about something? Could it be that it was harder than I thought to always have to be stylish and cool? Maybe knowing that everyone in the whole school was looking at them to set the trends all the time was a really big strain on them.

Of course, even if that was the truth, it was no excuse for the way they acted. They were never nice. Not for a second. Lots of people have problems and they don't say and do the horrible things Addie, Dana, and the rest of the Pops do, day in and day out. I put any feelings of understanding or pity for the Pops right out of my head.

Besides, I didn't feel like thinking about the Pops right now. I was on vacation from school *and* from them. I just wanted to be right where I was — at my friend Rachel's house, having hot chocolate and getting to know her cousin a little better. I had a feeling that Madison was going to turn out to be pretty cool after all. Just the way Rachel had promised she would be.

Chapter
NINE

MADISON REALLY CHANGED after our conversation. I knew she was still worried about her parents fighting a lot, but I could tell she felt better after confiding in me. And it turned out she was really a lot of fun. Like Rachel, she told a lot of jokes, but hers were usually a little funnier than her cousin's. And she was almost as good of a mimic as Chloe. She really cracked me up imitating the woman who does the weather on the local newscast. Madison would make her voice all deep and scratchy like the weathercaster's and then say, "The weather in Mexico City will be chili today, hot tamale," which I thought was hilarious.

My other friends seemed to like her better, too. Of course, they didn't understand the reason for the sudden transformation in her personality, but they didn't ask any questions. They were just relieved that she wasn't bringing everybody down anymore.

For the rest of the break, my friends and I took

Madison all over town — to the funplex for video games and pinball, to our favorite diner (the one that has little minijukeboxes at each table), and, of course, sledding. I was having a really good time. That is until two days before New Year's Eve, when I called Chloe to see what she was up to.

"What are you going to do this afternoon?" I asked her.

At first, there was dead silence on the phone. And then Chloe said, "I'm sort of going shopping."

"Sort of?" I asked her.

"Well, I mean, I . . . um . . . I'm definitely going shopping," Chloe told me.

Okay, this was weird. Chloe never seemed uncomfortable when she was talking to me. But today she really was being evasive.

Or maybe I was just imagining it. "I have some Christmas money that my aunt sent me. Do you want company while you shop?" I asked her.

Again, dead silence on the other end of the phone.

"Chloe?" I asked. "Are you still there?"

"Yeah, I'm here," she said slowly. "The thing is, Jen, you won't want to come shopping. I'm going with Rachel and Madison to buy something to wear to Marc's New Year's Eve party."

Now it was my turn to grow quiet. I'd almost managed to push the party out of my head over the past few days. But now Chloe had reminded me about it. And she was right. I didn't want to go and watch my friends buy outfits to wear to a party I hadn't been invited to.

"Okay," I told Chloe, trying really hard not to sound as upset as I was. "Well, you guys have fun, and maybe we can do something tomorrow instead."

"Sure," Chloe replied. "Tomorrow we'll do something really fun." She paused for a minute. "Jenny, are you sure you don't want to call Marc and just ask him . . ."

"I'm sure," I told her. "It's just one stupid night. Besides, my folks really want me to be here for our block's annual progressive dinner. It's a tradition."

"Okay," Chloe said. "Look, I have to run. Rachel's mom's picking me up in five minutes. I'll see you tomorrow."

"Yep, tomorrow," I said. As I hung up the phone I could feel the salty tears welling up. They burned my eyes as they overflowed onto my cheeks, and I didn't even try to stop them. What I needed right then and there was a good cry. So I let it happen.

Eventually, I stopped crying. I'd run out of tears, and my stomach was getting kind of sore from all the sobbing. I was really glad my mom had been all the way in the basement doing the laundry. I didn't want to have to explain to her the reason I'd been crying. It was just too embarrassing.

Once I stopped crying, I realized I didn't have anything to do. I thought about calling Liza, or Felicia, or the twins, and seeing what they were up to. But I had a feeling they were probably shopping, too. And I didn't want to feel even more left out than I already did.

Then, suddenly, I remembered that I did have one friend who wasn't going to Marc's party, either. Sam! I raced over to the computer, fingers crossed, hoping she was online. And sure enough she was. Immediately, I invited her to video chat. Of course she accepted. And when she appeared on the screen, I was never so glad to see a friendly face in my whole life.

"What's up, chum?" Sam asked me.

Her voice shocked me for a minute. Her accent was so thick. It was the way she sounded the first day she arrived at school.

"Nothing much," I told her. "I'm just hanging out here. I needed a rest. It's been crazy."

"It's been crazy here, too," Sam said. "Which is why I'm at my grandmum's cabbaging for a bit."

"Cabbaging?" I asked her.

"Mmhmm," Sam said. "You know, vegetating. Doing nothing."

"Oh right. Gotcha," I said. "How was your Christmas?"

"Amazing," she told me. "I went caroling with my friend Melanie. And she's such a mad alec. Everywhere we went she was doing cartwheels and headstands on the lawns while she sang. She put on a whole performance."

I wasn't exactly sure what a mad alec was, but from the sound of what Sam was saying, I suspected Melanie was sort of wild and crazy.

"And yesterday I took the tube with some of my friends and we went to this amazing flea market," Sam continued. "I got these socks. Aren't they brill?"

Sam held her legs up to the screen so I could see her mismatched knee socks. One sock was yellow with pink polka dots. The other was yellow, pink, and red striped.

"It sounds like you're having a really good time over there across the pond," I said, using an expression I'd heard Sam say a million times. The pond was the Atlantic Ocean.

"I am," Sam said. "Which is making it a lot easier for me."

"Making what a lot easier for you?" I asked her.

Sam stopped for a minute, realizing what she'd just said. "I wasn't going to say anything to any of you lot," she explained slowly. "At least not until I'm sure, which I'm not, so . . ."

"Not sure about what?" I asked. I was starting to get a nervous feeling in my stomach. Somehow I knew this conversation wasn't going to end well.

"Well, my mum and dad have been talking about moving back here," Sam told me. "Mum's so much happier near her parents. And Dad said he could try to get a job at the main office of his company here in London, rather than being at one of the smaller branches in the States, if it would make her happier."

If it would make her happier. I repeated the words over in my head. What about Sam's happiness? Didn't that count? And what about my happiness? Sam was one of my best friends. She'd just come into my life. I wasn't ready to lose her.

"But there's a chance you'll come back here, right?" I asked her.

"Sure, there's a chance," Sam said, noting the desperation in my voice. "Nothing's been settled yet. Mum's got a possibility of a job back in the States, too, and I'm not sure she'd want to start looking for work all over again here."

I smiled. There, that sounded more positive.

"I'll keep you posted, Jenny, I promise," Sam said. "But *you* have to promise me that you won't tell anyone about this. Everything's way too up in the air."

"It's a promise," I told her. And it was one I was sure I would keep. After all, no one was around for me to tell anything to. They were all shopping for Marc's party.

I sat there for a while feeling really sorry for myself. But that got boring. I wanted to do something. Anything. I had to get my mind off of my troubles. So I turned to my favorite website to cheer me up. I figured doing a fun quiz would make the time fly by.

There was a long list of quizzes to choose from.

I moved the cursor down the list, looking for something to grab my interest. Finally I found a quiz that seemed designed to brighten up anyone's day. And boy, did my day need brightening!

You're a Rainbow!

Have you ever been told that you have a colorful personality? Have you ever wondered what that means? Are you a mellow yellow, a groovy green, a raucous red, or a blissful blue? To find out, click your mouse and take this colorful quiz.

1. You've just had a major disagreement with your BFF. How would you best describe the way you behaved during the argument?

A. I ended up crying.

B. I yelled at her. I was mad!

C. I walked away. I hate confrontation.

D. I listened to what she had to say and then tried to talk things out with her.

Hmmm. This one was going to take some thought. I don't really have a BFF anymore. I have a lot of really close friends instead. It's just the way my group has always been. Still, at the moment I guess you could say I was in a fight with Marc. Or at least I was angry with him. And I had opted not to talk to him about it. Which meant that C was the most logical answer for me. So I clicked the letter C, and waited for the next question to pop up on the screen.

2. My idea of the perfect vacation is:

A. Getting to sleep late and watch old movies in bed.

B. Heading off to a big city for shopping and shows.

C. Camping and hiking in the woods.

D. Hanging out in a beach house with lots of friends and family.

Wow! Middleschoolsurvival.com quizzes could be really hard sometimes. There were so many different answers I could give to this one. Like, for instance, during this break I'd been sleeping late and watching a whole lot of TV. But I'd also been hanging out with lots of friends and family. Still, the best vacation I'd ever had was last summer when I went to sleepaway camp. And we did a lot of hiking and camping out (not to mention canoe trips, arts and crafts, and sports). So I clicked the letter C.

3. Which of these jobs most appeals to you?

A. Nurse.
B. Advertising executive.
C. Landscape designer.
D. Customer service manager.

Well, I knew the answer definitely wasn't A. I can't stand the sight of blood, or watching someone throw up, and I know nurses have to deal with that kind of stuff all the time. As for a landscape designer, I knew that one was out, because every time my dad asks me if I want to help him with the garden in our yard I find a million excuses not to.

So that left either an advertising executive or a customer service manager. Advertising seems like fun, coming up with jingles about candies or commercials for cars or something. But I'm not particularly musical, and everyone I know clicks through the commercials these days. So advertising didn't seem like a great career move.

On the other hand, I am really good at solving other people's problems, even if I'm not so fantastic at solving my own. I'd make a really great customer service manager. D was my answer, for sure.

A moment later, question number four appeared on my computer screen.

4. If you could take up any hobby, which would it be?

A. Ballet dancing.
B. Skydiving.
C. Gardening.
D. Playing softball.

Well C was out for sure. I wasn't any more into gardening now than I had been when I was answering question three. And I'd tried ballet once, when I was five. I was terrible at it. I just wasn't into dancing around the room pretending I was a fairy princess or a pony leaping over a fence. My idea of dancing is just moving to the music with my friends at a party or something.

As for skydiving, I knew that was out. My mom and dad would never let me jump out of airplanes for a hobby. No way! So that just left D, softball. I figured that could actually be kind of fun. Being on a team with a lot of other girls doing sports sounded like something I might want to do. So I clicked on the letter D. A moment later, the next question popped up on the screen.

5. You're at a party, and someone has just cranked up the tunes. Where can you be found?

A. Watching my friends dance.

B. Going crazy in the middle of the dance floor.

C. Leaving the room for a quieter, less crowded spot, where my friends and I can talk and hang out.

D. Trying to make a friend of mine feel more comfortable in the crowd.

This question didn't take a lot of thought on my part. I knew exactly what I would do. Hadn't I been the one to volunteer to help Madison learn to skate that day at the rink? And hadn't I been the one to talk to her at the twins' party? My answer was definitely D.

So, which color is your personality? To find out, check the chart.

You answered: C, C, D, D, D

Mostly A's: *Blue.* Like the blue sea, your emotions run deep. You are caring and kind, but also easily hurt by others who may be less sensitive.

Mostly B's: *Red.* You're a fiery girl who is driven by passion and lives for excitement.

Mostly C's: *Green.* You don't need a lot of people around to feel happy. In fact, you're at your best when you're alone communing with nature. The great outdoors makes you feel alive.

Mostly D's: *Yellow.* You tend to look at the sunny side of life. That optimistic outlook is what allows you to believe that there is good in everyone.

I stared at the screen for a few minutes, soaking in the information. *Yellow.* I liked that. Yellow always reminds me of sunshine, golden sunflowers, and happy things. Who wouldn't want to have a personality with those kinds of characteristics? The quiz was pretty right on about my personality, too. For the most part I can say that I'm optimistic, and I usually do try to see the good side in people. Well, maybe not as much as, say, Liza, who is probably the sunniest of my friends, but pretty much. I grinned as I turned off the computer and went downstairs for a snack. Once again, my number one website had managed to put me back in a good mood.

And that mood stuck with me. The next afternoon, I went to the movies with Chloe and her dad, which was a lot of fun. Chloe's dad is hilarious. He's really outgoing, and like Chloe, he's able to mimic just about anyone. So on the car ride home, I got to relive the entire movie all over again.

"I loved when the cat leaped out from behind the lamppost and scared the crook." Chloe giggled as we stopped at a red light.

"Aaaaahhhhh!" Chloe's dad screamed, throwing one hand way up in the air and tossing his head back, just like the actor in the movie had done.

"That's hilarious," I said from the backseat. I was laughing so hard my stomach hurt.

"And how about that woman sitting in the row in front of us?" Chloe asked me. "What was that hat she was wearing?"

I giggled. The woman in the row in front had been wearing this knit hat that seemed to have a whole village of little woolen dolls sewn onto it. It was definitely the weirdest looking hat I'd ever seen. And it was huge, too.

"Why do I always get the ones with the big hair or the big hats?" Chloe's dad asked.

"At least she moved over when you asked her to, Dad," Chloe reminded him. "It could have been worse."

"True," Chloe's dad agreed. "Someone could have given *me* that hat for Christmas."

The thought of Chloe's dad's big, bald head shoved into that ugly woolen hat was too much for me. I laughed so hard that I was out of breath when the car pulled up in front of my house.

"Thanks so much," I told Chloe's dad. "This was really fun." I turned to Chloe. "Well, since tomorrow's New Year's Eve, I guess I'll see you next year."

Chloe gave me a funny look. "Jen . . ." she began.

I smiled at her, refusing to be the one to break the bad mood. "It's really cool, Chloe," I told her. "I'm actually really looking forward to the progressive dinner."

"Okay," Chloe said. "Have a great time."

"I will," I assured her.

As I got out of the car, I promised myself that I would do exactly that. There were plenty of things to look forward to at the progressive dinner – great food, seeing the grown-ups looking ridiculous in party hats, and getting to stay up really late to watch the ball drop in Times Square on TV. Yep, I was going to have a really good – really *yellow* – time on New Year's Eve!

Chapter
TEN

I WOKE UP the next morning to the sound of my dad banging around pots and pans in the kitchen and my mom vacuuming the living room — just as I had done every New Year's Eve morning since I could remember. My parents were getting ready for the party. That meant for the rest of the day, I would have to stay out of the way. My parents are totally obsessive about their party planning. They'd been arguing over what hors d'oeuvres to serve all week long. Of course, I'd been part of that discussion several times. And I'm proud to say that the mini-pigs in a blanket and teeny-tiny potato knishes were my ideas. I knew no kids were going to want to chow down on stuffed mushrooms or spinach and cheese pies.

As part of my "staying out of the way" contribution to the party setup, I decided to try to video chat with Sam before going downstairs for breakfast. I wasn't exactly sure what time it was in

England right now, but I wanted to be sure that I could catch her before she went out to celebrate New Year's Eve. I really wanted to know what her parents had decided about moving back to England.

But when I tried to reach her, all I got was her away message. It read, "Sam is off to Spitalfields to find the perfect dress to ring in the New Year at Ian's party. Lots of news to celebrate this year. Cheers, mates!"

I stared at the message for a while, feeling confused. Sam had been gone less than two weeks, but already there was so much going on in her life that I didn't know anything about. For one thing, what was Spitalfields? And who was Ian? And most important, what was her big news? Was it that she was staying in England for good, and she was happy about it? Or was it something else? Something that I would want to celebrate, too? Like the fact that she was coming back to the States?

I knew I wasn't going to be able to figure it all out just from what she'd written there. But I did want Sam to know that I was thinking about her. So I sent her an e-mail that read, "Happy New Year, Sam. What's the big news? Zap me an e-mail, okay? <3 Jenny."

Then I went downstairs to try to figure out how to make myself breakfast and stay out of my parents' way at the same time.

By six o'clock, our house was spotless and all set up for the progressive party. The cheese and crackers were on the table. The spinach pies, knishes, and pigs in a blanket were in the oven, and I had finally decided on an outfit after trying on about six different pairs of jeans and about a dozen sweaters. I figured that just because I wasn't going to Marc's party didn't mean I couldn't look cool.

"You look so cute, Jen-Jen," my mom said as I came down the stairs in my lemon yellow sweater and skinny blue jeans.

My mood automatically fell. The word *cute* can do that to a person, especially when a parent says it. Did you ever notice that if your friends tell you you look cute, it's a compliment, but if your mom tells you the same thing, it makes you feel like you're five years old again?

I thought about going upstairs and changing before everyone arrived, but I was too late. Before I could turn around and head for my room, the doorbell rang.

"Jenny, can you get that?" my mother asked me. "I'm going to run and set up the Shirley Temple drinks for the kids."

That sounded pretty good to me. I love Shirley Temples. They're really just lemon-lime soda and red grenadine, but my mom serves them in pretty glasses with a cherry in each one, so they look really sophisticated. And they taste really great.

I wasn't exactly sure how many Shirley Temples mom was going to have to make, though. We don't have a whole lot of kids in our neighborhood anymore. At least not kids who would come to a family New Year's Eve party. A lot of the bigger kids who used to come to our parties were teenagers now, and I figured they would have plans of their own. And the really little kids usually drank from their juice cups. In the past, that had left a whole lot of Shirley Temple drinks for Addie and me. But this year, I suspected the Pops were having their own New Year's party at someone's house. Why wouldn't they? My crowd of friends were having one, weren't they?

"Hi, Jenny," Mrs. Henderson from down the block said as she and her husband came into the house.

"Hello," I replied.

"Jenny, can you hang everyone's coats in the hall closet?" my mom said as she put the tray of Shirley Temples on the dining room table and made her way to the living room to greet our guests.

I don't know why my mother wanted me to bother hanging up coats. Since this was a progressive party, we'd all be putting them on again in about an hour when it was time to move to the next house for the next course. But I didn't argue. I just took Mr. and Mrs. Henderson's wool coats and hung them up.

And as soon as I did that, the bell rang again. This time there was a whole crowd of people standing on our porch. The people in my neighborhood are nothing if not punctual. No one's ever late — especially when there's food involved.

I've spent my entire life in this house, and I know everyone in the neighborhood, so there were no strangers or surprise guests on the porch when I opened the door. At least not at first. But as the neighbors began to come inside, I noticed two stragglers lagging behind on my front lawn. And they were definitely a surprise.

"Addie and Dana!" I exclaimed. The minute the names left my lips I wished I could choke them back. I hadn't meant to sound surprised or excited.

The words had just popped out. Those two were the last people I expected to see at a neighborhood party on New Year's Eve. Especially since Addie's parents were here, too. The Pops always made it a point to never go anywhere that their parents were going. But now, here they were, at a party with Addie's parents. I guess Addie had dragged Dana along so she wouldn't have to be alone with the adults — or have to talk to me.

"I'm surprised to see you guys," I told them as they slowly walked through the door.

"I'm pretty surprised to see you, too," Addie said.

"I thought you'd be at the dweeb party your friend Marc is throwing," Dana added.

I turned beet red at the very mention of Marc's party. It was bad enough that I wasn't invited. But knowing that the Pops knew about it, too, was absolutely unbearable. Once again, I could feel salty tears beginning to burn in my eyes.

"H-h-how did you know about Marc's party?" I stammered, fighting back the tears. I was absolutely not going to cry about this in front of Dana and Addie. No how. No way.

"*Everybody* knows about it," Dana said. She

looked at Addie and began to laugh. "Those geeky invitations with the streamers and balloons all over them. They looked like something for a nursery school birthday party."

Now I was really freaking out. If Dana knew what Marc's invitation looked like, it meant she must have gotten one. Marc had invited Dana and not me! It was getting almost impossible to hold back the tears.

"Seriously, Jenny," Addie said. "Why aren't you at the party?"

I didn't know what to say. I couldn't just come out and admit to two of my worst enemies that one of my supposed friends had totally dissed me by not inviting me.

"Why aren't *you* there?" I shot back, not knowing what else to say.

"I wasn't invited," Addie said. "Why would I be? But you were invited. So I figured that was where you'd be."

I looked at her strangely. "Why would you assume that I was invited?"

"Because he's one of your friends," Addie said in a voice tinged with more than a little disdain. "And because . . ."

I saw Dana poke Addie in the ribs, and she stopped midsentence. Then the two of them burst out laughing.

"What's so funny?" I demanded. I could feel the anger rising in me, and my voice was suddenly a lot louder than I'd planned. A few of the adults turned to stare at us.

Addie must have spotted the adults looking in our direction, because she lowered her voice when she answered me. "Don't tell me you didn't know."

"Know what?" I asked her.

"That someone took the invitation off your locker before you got there," Addie replied.

"How do *you* know that?" I demanded.

"Because Dana's the one who took it," she said matter-of-factly, as though stealing someone else's party invitation was the most normal thing in the world.

Dana stared at Addie. "I can't believe you just told her that."

"She would have figured it out, anyway," Addie told Dana. Then she looked at me. "I can't believe you didn't figure it out already. What did Marc say when you asked him where your invitation was?"

I didn't know how to answer that. For one thing, I was in absolute shock. And for another, Marc hadn't said anything, because I *hadn't* asked him about my invitation. Instead, I'd just been avoiding him the whole break.

How dumb was I? Even *Addie* had assumed that Marc and I were close enough friends for me to go and talk to him if I was upset about something. Chloe had felt the same way. If only I had listened to Chloe and talked to Marc before school let out. I would have had such a better holiday break. I could have kicked myself.

I wasn't just mad at myself, though. I was plenty mad at Dana, too. But there was no way I was going to let her know that she had ruined a good part of my break. That would just give her satisfaction.

So instead, I just said, "I . . . um . . . I didn't know who took my invitation." It wasn't a lie. After all, I didn't know I had been given an invitation, so how could I know who stole it?

"You still didn't answer my question," Addie said. "Why aren't you at Marc's?"

"I . . . um . . . I will be," I told her. "After this part of the party. I didn't think it would be right to miss the appetizers, since they're at my house and all. Besides, my mom needed my help with the coats."

I didn't say anything to Addie and Dana after

that. My mind was racing a mile a minute. I couldn't believe what Dana had done to me by stealing my invitation. She'd practically stolen the whole Christmas vacation from me. Or at least the part of it I'd wasted being angry with Marc.

Marc was probably really confused, too. He'd had no idea why I had been so cold to him over break. And I *had* been pretty frosty toward him. I was always walking away when I saw him, and dismissing pretty much everything he had to say.

I had to fix this, right away! Quickly, I ran off to find one of my parents. I needed them to do me a huge favor.

"That was a cruel thing for Dana to do to you," my mother said as she drove me to Marc's house about a half an hour later. We'd left the minute the appetizer portion of the progressive dinner party had ended. I didn't even take the time to change into a skirt, even though I knew my other friends would be wearing dresses. (Well, not Josh and Marc, of course.) I just wanted to get there!

"Dana's pretty cruel all of the time," I told my mom. I shifted slightly in my seat. It was kind of uncomfortable talking to her about all the social stuff at school.

"At least Addie let you in on Dana's secret," my mom continued. "That was nice of her. Deep down, I think you guys are still friends."

It was statements like that which made me feel weird talking to my mom about the Pops. She really didn't understand at all. Addie wasn't my friend, not one bit. If she had really been a friend she would have stopped Dana from stealing the invitation in the first place. Or she would have told me about it a lot sooner, like when we were in the car going home from the skating rink together. But she hadn't. She'd let me go on thinking I was the only one not invited to the party.

Still, at least I knew about the stolen invitation now. And I was on the way to Marc's party. I would apologize to him for being a jerk, and hopefully he would forgive me. I was pretty sure he would. Marc's like me. He doesn't want to lose any of his good friends. And since I had a feeling we might all be losing Sam, it was more important than ever that the rest of us stick together.

"Can't you drive a little faster?" I urged my mom. "I've already missed an hour of the party."

"Relax, Jenny," my mom said. "It's a long time until midnight. You've got plenty of time to have fun with your friends."

Chapter
ELEVEN

"DANA IS SUCH A JERK," Marc declared after I'd arrived at the party and explained everything.

"You're stating the obvious," Chloe teased him. Then she turned to me. "I told you so," she added.

I nodded. "You were right."

"Again, stating the obvious," Chloe told me. "I'm always right."

"Well, you were right this time, anyway," I replied. "She said I just should have asked you where my invitation was," I explained to Marc.

Marc shrugged. "I can see where that might have been awkward."

"I'm just glad you're not mad at me for being kind of mean over the break," I told him.

"I'm just glad you're not mad at me," Marc said. "I couldn't figure out what I'd done wrong."

"That's because you *didn't* do anything wrong," I told him. "*Dana* did."

"Well, you're here now, and you have perfect timing," Liza said, steering me over to the big table Marc's mom had set up in the basement. "The pizza just arrived."

"Mmm . . . pepperoni. My favorite," I said, taking a big slice and putting it on a plate.

"It's ours, too!" Marilyn and Carolyn said at the same time.

"I think this is the best pizza I've ever had," Madison added. "It's so much cheesier than the pizza near my house."

Rachel flashed a mischievous smile at her cousin. "Do you know which side of the pizza is the left side?"

"Nope, which one?" Madison asked.

"The side that hasn't been eaten yet!" Rachel exclaimed. Then she began to laugh at her own joke.

Madison laughed, too. "That was hilarious," she said.

Felicia looked from Rachel to Madison and back again. "A really bad sense of humor must run in the family," she teased.

"I had no idea that was genetic," Josh agreed. "But you must be right."

Rachel threw a kernel of popcorn at Felicia and Josh and laughed even harder.

"I'm so glad we're all here together at a party on New Year's Eve," Chloe told me.

"Well, most of us, anyway," I pointed out.

"Who's missing?" Madison asked. She turned to Rachel. "I thought I knew all of your friends."

"Not Sam," Rachel explained. "She's in England."

Madison looked at me. "I thought you said Sam was your mouse, and he lived in your room."

I laughed. "There are two Sams. Well, actually one Sam, and one *Samantha*. Samantha's the one in England." I frowned slightly, thinking about the secret Sam had shared with me on the computer. Now I really understood why Madison had had a hard time when she'd first come to town. Keeping a rotten secret all to yourself really wears you down.

"Sam's from England," Rachel explained to her cousin. "But she lives here now. I'm not sure when she's coming home. Maybe you'll still be here when she does."

"Has anyone talked to her?" Liza asked. "Did she say when she was coming back?"

"I talked to her the other day," I answered. "She told me she was going to a party at her friend Ian's tonight, and that she'd been doing a lot of shopping. But she didn't say what her plans were about coming home. At least not for sure."

Liza looked at me curiously, but didn't say anything. The other kids apparently hadn't noticed the slightly tense tone in my voice. But Liza had. She's sensitive to things like that.

"Let's ask her!" Chloe announced suddenly. She walked over to the desk in the back corner of the basement and turned on the computer.

"Chloe, do you have any idea what time it is over there?" Liza asked her.

"Probably around one or two o'clock in the morning," Chloe admitted. "But I think she's going to be up. It's New Year's Eve."

"How weird," Madison said. "It's already next year over there."

Wow. Madison was right. And thinking that Sam was a year ahead of us already made her seem farther away than ever.

Chloe checked the list of Marc's friends who were online. Sam's name was right near the top. "See, I told you," she said, clicking on the chat button.

A moment later, Sam's face appeared on the screen. She was obviously getting ready for bed, because she was wearing flannel pajamas and had her hair clipped back. But she looked wide-awake, and judging from the smile on her face, I could tell she was happy to have heard from us.

"Hi!" Sam said. "Happy New Year."

"We still have a few hours to go," Chloe reminded her. "But Happy New Year to you."

"Thanks," Sam said. "I just got back from a great party at my friend Ian's house."

"I know," Chloe told her. "Jenny told us." She paused for a minute. "But she said she didn't know when you were coming home. We just wanted to find out, because Rachel's cousin Madison wants to meet you."

Madison stuck her face in front of the camera. "Hi, Sam," she said.

"Hi, Madison," Sam replied. "Are you having fun?"

"Totally," Madison said cheerfully. "Your friends are really great."

"I know. I can't wait to get home to them," Sam told her.

Now it was my turn to stick my face in front of the camera. "So you're coming back?" I asked her excitedly.

My friends all stared at me. They were definitely confused.

"Of course she's coming back," Chloe said. "Why wouldn't she be?"

"My mum got sort of homesick for England when we got here," Sam explained. "She wanted to stay. At least she thought she did."

Liza looked at me. "You knew about this and you didn't tell anyone?" she asked me.

"I asked her not to," Sam said quickly. "And now I'm glad she didn't, because it's not going to happen."

"So when are you coming back?" I asked excitedly. I was in such a great mood. This night was definitely turning out a whole lot better than I'd expected it to!

"I fly back in two days," Sam told us. "Mum got a call from the States just this morning telling her that she'd gotten the job she was up for back in the States, and Dad realized that the job here wasn't nearly as great as the one he has over there. It all sort of happened very quickly. So I guess I'm still stuck with you lot." She said that last part with a huge grin on her face.

"So what was the big news you had to celebrate at Ian's party?" I asked her.

"Oh that," Sam said. "It wasn't about me. My friend Feeny — well, we call her Feeny but her name's really Stephanie — anyway, Feeny just got into this really incredible middle school that she's been dying to transfer into. So my gang here was celebrating that."

I grinned broadly. I was very happy for Feeny, even if I'd never met her. But I was even happier for us. Sam wasn't going to disappear from our lives after all. "We're all going to be together in the New Year!" I exclaimed.

"Too bad we're not all together tonight," Marilyn said.

"You're missing a great party," Carolyn added.

"She doesn't have to miss it," I pointed out to my friends. They all just sort of stared at me. I think they thought I'd gone nuts.

"It's a little late for her to fly back for the party," Marc said.

I laughed. "I know. But if we leave the computer on, she can see the party, and we can talk to her. It'll be just like she's here."

"That's true," Sam agreed. "I can be your virtual guest."

"Exactly," I agreed.

"It's just a bummer that we can't send you virtual pizza," Chloe told her. "This slice is delicious."

Everyone laughed at that. And as I looked around the room at my friends laughing, talking, eating, and generally having a good time, I realized that the Pops were no longer a threat. Sure they were mean and cruel, and they tended to play jokes that could make you miserable once in a while. But while they might steal invitations from me, they couldn't take away the most important thing I needed in order to survive middle school: my friends. They were here for me, and I was there for them. And in the end, that was all that mattered.

Are You a Gracious Gift Getter?

Everyone says it is better to give than to receive. The question is, how do you behave when you're on the receiving end of that equation? Are you gracious or greedy? There's only one way to find out. You've got to take the quiz.

1. **It's been a tough year for your family in the money department. This year, your parents let you know that you will be getting fewer gifts than usual for Christmas. How do you react?**

   A. You tell them you understand that money's been tight.

   B. You are MAD! After all, other families have money issues, but their kids are still hauling in the loot.

   C. You suggest that this year your family give homemade gifts to one another.

2. Your art club is doing a Secret Snowflake week and you find out your gifts have been coming from the group geek. How do you react?

A. You make a face and let your friends know you think all the gifts have been hideous.

B. Say thank you.

C. Let her know how much you appreciate the effort she put into finding the right gifts for you.

3. Yikes! Grandma bought you a really ugly blouse for your birthday. What do you do?

A. Suggest the two of you go shopping together so she can see what your taste is like.

B. Thank her for the lovely gift, and make sure you wear it when she can see you in it.

C. Thank her for the gift, and then conveniently bury it in your closet.

4. Your mom insists you write thank-you notes for all your holiday gifts. When do you get them done?

A. By the end of your winter break.

B. When your mom finally gets mad enough to type out a note you can print out a bunch of times and just sign your name at the bottom.

C. Before spring.

5. You receive a holiday gift from someone you are friendly with but not particularly close to. It never occurred to you to get her one. How do you react?

  A. Say you love what she got you, even if you don't.
  B. Refuse the gift.
  C. Thank her and let her know how much you appreciate the gesture.

6. You and your sister both get Christmas gifts from your parents. But looking at them it's easy to tell hers cost a lot more than yours. What do you do?

  A. Keep your disappointment to yourself.
  B. Ask your parents why they like her more.
  C. Forget about it. It's the thought — not the price — that counts.

7. You've been hinting to your BFF that you want a special pair of earrings for your birthday. But she shows up at your party with a CD you already own. How do you react?

  A. You thank her for remembering who your favorite band is, and then later exchange the gift without her knowing.
  B. You make a mental note to get her something she doesn't really want for her birthday.
  C. You say a simple thank you, and then unwrap the next gift.

8. **It's Christmas morning, and when you look under the tree you do not find that new winter jacket you've been eyeing. What do you do?**

A. Open all your gifts, and say thank you. Then count up your Christmas cash to see if you have enough to buy that jacket.

B. Forget about the jacket. After all, there are so many other cool gifts in those boxes.

C. Ask your parents why they never listen to you when you tell them what you really want.

Now it's time to add up your score.

1. A. 2 points   B. 1 point   C. 3 points
2. A. 1 point   B. 2 points C. 3 points
3. A. 1 point   B. 3 points C. 2 points
4. A. 2 points   B. 3 points C. 1 point
5. A. 3 points   B. 1 point   C. 2 points
6. A. 2 points   B. 1 point   C. 3 points
7. A. 3 points   B. 1 point   C. 2 points
8. A. 2 points   B. 3 points C. 1 point

So what does your score say about you?

8-12 points: It seems like it's your friends and family who have been on the receiving end — of your bad attitude. Remember when someone gives you a gift, it's a signal they've been thinking about you. So it's important that you think about their feelings when you receive that gift. It's not that hard to say thank you.

13-18 points: You understand the importance of a polite thank you, even if you don't always feel like giving thanks. Basically, you're an average kid, with above-average manners. Kudos!

19-24 points: You have a unique gift (pun intended!) — the ability to make others feel special and appreciated. Thank *you* for your kindness.

Here's a sneak peek at Jenny's next middle school adventure!

As soon as the bus pulled up to my stop, I hurried off and raced the two blocks to my house. Then I burst through the front door.

"I'm home, Mom!" I shouted. "Where's the surprise?"

"We're in the kitchen!" my mother called back.

We're? Was that some sort of clue? "Who's we?" I called.

"Come see," my mother said playfully.

I zoomed through the living room straight to the kitchen. And there, sitting in the seat my dad usually sits in was my surprise.

"Aunt Amy!" I exclaimed. Then I ran over and gave her a huge hug.

"Hi to you, too," my aunt laughed.

"I can't believe you're here!" I squealed joyfully.

"I have some time off, so I figured I'd come visit my favorite niece."

I laughed. "I'm your *only* niece," I reminded her.

"Even if your mom had a dozen kids, you'd still be my favorite," Aunt Amy assured me.

I smiled. Aunt Amy always knew exactly the right thing to say. She was incredible and really fun to be around. She was one of the most exciting people I knew, which is why I was kind of surprised she was in my hometown. Life around here isn't exactly exciting.

"You had time off and you wanted to spend it *here?*" I asked her. "It's so boring here. And you live in New York City. There must be a million fun things to do there while you are on vacation. Like you could go to the Empire State Building, or Broadway, or the Statue of Liberty or . . ."

Aunt Amy shook her head. "I'm flying off to China on business a week from Saturday, and I thought I could use a few quiet, restful days here with you guys first. Besides, I *live* in New York. I walk past the Empire State Building every day on the way from the subway to my office, and I can see the Statue of Liberty from my apartment window. I'd rather vacation here and hang out with you and your mice."

I grinned. Most adults hated my two pet white mice. Even my mom wasn't exactly crazy about them. But Aunt Amy *liked* mice. In fact, she was always saying that one day she was going to create a whole line of greeting cards with pictures of them on the front.

That's what my aunt does. She's the art director for the Connections Greeting Card Company. She flies all over the world, meeting artists and checking on the factories where the cards are manufactured. That was probably why she was flying to China — a lot of the company's greeting cards are printed overseas. My Aunt Amy definitely has a very exciting career.

Career! Suddenly I smiled broadly. Now I was doubly glad Aunt Amy had arrived. "Are you still going to be in town on Tuesday?" I asked her.

Aunt Amy took a sip of her coffee and nodded. "Mmhmm. My flight's not until a week from Saturday."

"Great!" I exclaimed.

"Why?" Aunt Amy asked.

"Well, Career Day at my school is on Tuesday, and since I'm on the student council I have to bring someone," I explained. "Aunt Amy, your job is *really* interesting. And since you're on vacation, you won't have to ask your boss for a day off so you can come."

"That's true," Aunt Amy said. "I'm free as a bird."

"Then you'll do it?" I asked her.

"Definitely," Aunt Amy said with a grin. "Anything for my Jennifer Juniper."

I smiled at my favorite aunt's nickname for me.

Then I said, "Aunt Amy, can I ask you one more favor?"

"What?"

"Please don't call me that at school."

Aunt Amy chuckled. "No problem — *Jenny*."

Will Jenny survive middle school?
Read these books to find out!

#1 Can You Get an F in Lunch?
Jenny's best friend, Addie, dumps her
on the first day of middle school.

#2 Madame President
Jenny and Addie both run for
class president. Who will win?

#3 I Heard a Rumor
The school gossip columnist
is revealing everyone's secrets!

#4 The New Girl
There's a new girl in school!
Will she be a Pop or not?

#5 Cheat Sheet
Could one of Jenny's friends
be a cheater?

#6 P.S. I Really Like You
Jenny has a secret admirer!
Who could it be?

Candy Apple Books

Drama Queen

I've Got a Secret

Confessions of a
Bitter Secret Santa

The Boy Next Door

The Sweetheart Deal

The Sister Switch

Snowfall Surprise

The Accidental
Cheerleader

The Babysitting Wars

Star-Crossed

Read them all!

Accidentally
Fabulous

Accidentally
Famous

Accidentally
Fooled

Accidentally
Friends

How to Be a Girly Girl
in Just Ten Days

Miss Popularity

Miss Popularity
Goes Camping

Making Waves

Life, Starring Me!

Juicy Gossip

Callie for President

Totally Crushed

Log on to my favorite website!
www.middleschoolsurvival.com

You'll find:
- Cool Polls and Quizzes
- Tips and Advice
- Message Boards
- And Everything Else You Need to Survive Middle School!